"You always we̶̶̶̶̶̶̶̶̶̶ Like those Raphae̶̶̶̶

"You mean the o̶̶̶̶ painting, looking

"Looking wistful," ̶̶̶ rected. "You always stuck your hand in your hair when you were studying, and your hair was always messy by the end of the day. It's one of the things that made me fall for you."

He smiled. "Apparently the cherubs were based on the children of Raphael's model for the Madonna. He painted them exactly as he saw them."

She rolled her eyes. "Trust you to know that."

He spread his hands. "What can I say? I've always had nerd tendencies."

That was something else she'd liked about him.

The only answer she had was to reach up and touch her mouth to his.

He wrapped his arms around her and kissed her all the way back.

She'd forgotten how it felt to kiss Angelo: the warmth, the sweetness, the coil of desire in her stomach that tightened and grew hotter.

When he finally broke the kiss, Sam's head was spinning and Angelo looked dazed.

"Sam…"

"I know." She traced his lower lip with the tip of her finger. "Me, too."

Dear Reader,

What happens when you unexpectedly meet with "the one who got away"?

Reunion stories can be tricky to write—the reasons why your hero and heroine break up need to be believable, but not something so tricky that they can't find a resolution and a way back to each other when they meet again. I hope you'll sympathize with Angelo struggling to do the right thing—and with Sam learning to trust him again!

I'm fascinated by advances in medicine, like operating in the womb, so I couldn't resist setting this book in a fetal medicine unit.

I've missed travel during the COVID years, so I also couldn't resist setting the book in a city I thoroughly enjoyed visiting: Florence.

I hope you enjoy their journey and a summer in Tuscany.

With love,

Kate Hardy

SURGEON'S SECOND CHANCE IN FLORENCE

KATE HARDY

MEDICAL ROMANCE

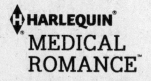

HARLEQUIN®
MEDICAL
ROMANCE™

Recycling programs
for this product may
not exist in your area.

ISBN-13: 978-1-335-40933-1

Surgeon's Second Chance in Florence

Harlequin Enterprises ULC
22 Adelaide St. West, 41st Floor
Toronto, Ontario M5H 4E3, Canada
www.Harlequin.com

Printed in U.S.A.

Kate Hardy has always loved books and could read before she went to school. She discovered Harlequin books when she was twelve and decided that this was what she wanted to do. When she isn't writing, Kate enjoys reading, cinema, ballroom dancing and the gym. You can contact her via her website, katehardy.com.

Books by Kate Hardy

Harlequin Medical Romance

Twin Docs' Perfect Match

Second Chance with Her Guarded GP
Baby Miracle for the ER Doc

Changing Shifts

Fling with Her Hot-Shot Consultant

Miracles at Muswell Hill Hospital

Christmas with Her Daredevil Doc
Their Pregnancy Gift

Carrying the Single Dad's Baby
Heart Surgeon, Prince…Husband!
A Nurse and a Pup to Heal Him
Mistletoe Proposal on the Children's Ward
Forever Family for the Midwife

Visit the Author Profile page
at Harlequin.com for more titles.

With love and thanks to the three editors
who worked with me on this book—
Julia, I'll miss you;
Megan, thank you for caretaking;
Laurie, welcome back!

**Praise for
Kate Hardy**

"Ms. Hardy has definitely penned a fascinating
read in this book… Once the hero confesses to the
heroine his plan for a marriage of convenience, I
was absolutely hooked."

—*Harlequin Junkie* on
Heart Surgeon, Prince…Husband!

CHAPTER ONE

'SAMANTHA CLARKE! JUST the woman I wanted to see.' Will Reynolds, the head of the department, smiled at Sam. 'Can we have a quick word in my office?'

Sam, assuming that her boss wanted her to talk to her about a new case, smiled back and followed him to his office.

'Have a seat,' he said, perching on the edge of his desk. 'First of all, I have some good news—that research grant we applied for has been confirmed, and we can start in three months' time. I'm delighted to say it means we'll be promoting you to consultant.'

Sam beamed at him. 'Thank you, Will! That's fantastic.'

'I knew you'd be pleased,' Will said. 'And, secondly, I have an interesting case for you. Triplet pregnancy from IVF—twins and a singleton.'

That was unusual enough in itself, but Sam

guessed there would also be a complication which might need surgery, or Will wouldn't be talking to her about it.

'And there's suspected twin-to-twin transfusion syndrome,' he said, confirming her thoughts.

'What stage?' she asked.

'They're doing another scan today at her hospital,' he said. 'If it's still stage two—' which Sam knew was when you couldn't see the smaller baby's bladder on the ultrasound, but it hadn't progressed to abnormal blood flow in the vessels around the heart '—then obviously amnioreduction is a possibility.'

When babies were still mildly affected by TTTS, doctors could try draining the excess fluid from one amniotic sac to resolve the problem. 'But you're thinking it's more likely to have progressed further and we'll need to do endoscopic laser ablation?' Sam had been working more intensively with foetal laser surgery over the last few months, so it sounded as if this was a mum and three babies who'd end up under her care.

'Got it in one,' he said.

'OK. When are they coming in?'

'That's the catch,' he said. 'They're not coming here.'

'So you're sending me to a different hospital in London?'

'Nope.' He wrinkled his nose. 'You know that the Muswell Hill Memorial Hospital is twinned with the Michelangelo Hospital in Florence?' At her nod, Will continued, 'Ricardo Fanelli, who's my equivalent in Florence, is setting up a new unit in foetal medicine. Professor Henri Lefevre from Paris is going to Florence for three months to oversee the unit and start training them, but Ric has asked for you to go over and treat this particular mum and her babies and work on secondment there until the research project starts.'

It was a fabulous opportunity, plus she'd always wanted to visit Florence.

Sam quickly suppressed the memory of the last time she'd visited Italy—and the last person she'd visited Italy with. That part of her life was over. Besides, as far as she knew, Angelo lived in Rome, so she was hardly likely to cross paths with him in Florence.

'Sam?'

She shook herself. Angelo had nothing to do with this. This was work. 'I'd love to do it, Will. When do they want me to start?'

'That's the other thing.' He wrinkled his nose. 'How's your Italian?'

'Conversational rather than medical,' she said. 'And it's horribly rusty.' She hadn't spoken Italian in two years, since Angelo had dumped her.

'They can probably help you with a translator, at least to start with,' Will said. 'But I'd advise you to get an app or something and start brushing it up again, and learning a few medical terms, because they want you to start on Thursday morning.'

'Thursday?' She felt her eyes widen. 'As in three days from now?'

'I know it's practically no notice, but that's when the mum's coming in again for another review,' he said.

'Well, that flat I was buying fell through, so I'm still staying with my parents. As long as you can cover me here, and I can get a flight, and someone in Florence doesn't mind helping me to find somewhere to stay, then...' She shrugged. 'I'm good to go.'

'That's great,' Will said. 'Though, as I said, I want you back for that research project. So no getting swept off your feet by a gorgeous Italian doctor, OK?'

Been there, done that, and won't make the same mistake again, Sam thought. 'No chance of that,' she said with a smile. 'If you don't mind me taking my break early, I need to tell my mum and sort out my flight.'

'Great. I'll ring Ric and tell him the good news,' Will said.

'Stop *worrying*. I'm perfectly fine,' Ruggiero Brunelli said.

Angelo wasn't entirely sure his dad was telling the truth. A visit every other week and a video call every day didn't feel like enough support. He loved living in Florence, but maybe he should move back to Rome to be closer to his dad?

'Angelo. You're the best son anyone could ask for,' Ruggiero said gently. 'And I'm not going to have a relapse. I'm eating properly, I go swimming three times a week, I see friends regularly, and I have Baffi to keep me company.' He gestured to the black and white cat who was snoozing in a patch of sunlight.

'I know.' But Angelo still worried. His father's addiction to painkillers had turned Angelo's life upside down two years ago. Angelo had been in England at the time, and on the cusp of asking Sam to marry him. But when his Uncle Salvatore had called to put him in the picture, Angelo had known he needed to move back to Italy and concentrate on helping his dad. And there was no way he could've dragged

Sam into it. Even if he'd ignored the potential scandal of a senior doctor self-prescribing narcotics—something that would've got Ruggiero struck off the register—there was the addiction side of things. Sam's younger brother had been an addict, and he'd died from an accidental overdose; she'd still been grieving when Angelo had first met her. How could he have asked her to support him through his dad's rehab, and bring all those painful memories back for her? Especially because he'd missed all the signs; how could he trust himself with her heart, when he'd let his dad down?

To protect her, he'd pushed her away—knowing that he was hurting her, but also knowing that if she stayed with him the situation would hurt her even more. And in a way, it had protected him as well; he'd felt helpless when he'd lost his mum, whereas ending it with Sam meant that at least he was in control. He'd done his best to minimise the potential hurt for both of them. Even though it had ripped his own heart out, lying to her and saying that he didn't love her any more.

He'd spent a year in Rome, supporting his father through the miserable months of rehab and then he'd been offered the job in Florence. He hadn't managed to persuade his dad to come with him and make a fresh start, but

Ruggiero had encouraged him to take the job. And at least the hour and a half on the train between Florence and Rome was quicker and easier than doing the train-plane-train trek from London.

'I still wish you'd move to Florence,' he said. 'We could get a house in the hills so you have a garden. And it's probably the best place in Italy for art. You know how much you loved visiting the Uffizi with me.'

'I was born in Rome and I'll die in Rome,' Ruggiero said.

Angelo thought of the car crash that had left his father hooked on heavy-duty painkillers. How easy it could've been for his dad to forget how much he'd taken, accidentally overdose and die, the way Sam's brother had. Or was this his father's way of telling Angelo he'd had enough of living on his own and wanted to be with Angelo's mum? He winced. '*Dad.*'

'I didn't mean it like that.' Ruggiero returned the wince. 'Sorry. Let me make it clear. I'm absolutely not suicidal and I'm not going to take an overdose, accidental or otherwise. I simply meant I'm stubborn, I love my home city and I plan to stay right where I am. I'm *fine*, son. Really.'

Though Angelo couldn't help running through a mental checklist: sweating, dilated or pinpoint pupils, co-ordination problems, itching…

His father was scratching his arm.

Ruggiero rolled his eyes as if he'd guessed what was going through Angelo's head. 'Pruritis has quite a few probable causes. Mine happens to be from an insect bite. See?' He held his arm so Angelo could see the reddened lump. 'Yes, I know scratching a bite is the quickest way to get it infected. I'm going to put a cold compress on it to stop the itching, after you've gone. And, no, I'm not going to take ibuprofen to reduce the swelling. I've got some antihistamine cream somewhere.' He gave Angelo a gentle smile. 'I might be ancient and two years out of practising medicine, but I can still just about remember my training.'

'Sorry, Dad.' Shame mingled with relief. 'You've got thirty years more experience than I have in medicine.'

'I made very a stupid mistake. I should've asked for help instead of thinking I could sort things out myself. And I've learned from that mistake,' Ruggiero said. 'When you come to see me, I really would like to see my son the man, rather than my son the doctor. I'd like to go out with you for good food and a glass of wine and tell you terrible jokes, and not have to worry that you're worrying about me.' He paused. 'And I'd like you to come to spend time with your dad, not to visit a patient who might lapse back into his painkiller addiction and needs watching like a hawk.'

Guilt surged through Angelo. 'I know. I want that, too.'

'But you still worry about me, whatever I say.' Ruggiero gave him a hug. 'It's supposed to be the other way round, you know, with the parent never stopping worrying about their child. You had the worry of your mum's breast cancer through your student years, and now it's me. Though, actually, I worry about you. I think you need someone in your life, Angelo: a partner, not a difficult parent.'

'You're not difficult,' Angelo said.

'If you weren't worrying about me, you'd relax,' Ruggiero pointed out. 'You'd date someone for more than a couple of months before backing off. You'd let someone close.'

Except Angelo knew that whoever he dated would never measure up to Sam. And he'd left it way too late to fix things between them. He'd learned that the hard way when he'd gone back to London. 'I'm fine,' Angelo lied.

'Hmm.' Ruggiero looked at him. 'If you're worrying that I wouldn't accept a male partner, then let me reassure you that I don't care whether you're gay, straight or somewhere in between. That doesn't matter. I just want you to be happy—and to be *loved*.'

Angelo blinked back the tears that unexpectedly stung his eyes. 'For the record, Dad, I'm straight. But I'm glad you'd accept me if I wasn't. I've seen friends go through a rough time until their families accepted who they were—even now.'

'Love is love,' Ruggiero said. 'Being a recovering addict has taught me a lot about acceptance. About not judging. And I want you to have a *life*, Angelo.'

'I do have a life,' Angelo protested. 'I have a job I love, good friends, and a flat with an amazing view.' Which was all true. Provided you didn't look beyond the surface to see the empty spaces.

'But you spend your time worrying about me instead of embracing life. You keep yourself at a distance from people,' Ruggiero said. 'So let's do a deal. I promise that I'll keep going to the addiction support group every week, and they have my full permission to contact you if they're even the slightest bit worried about me. Your uncle keeps an eye on me, too. And you—you make sure you date someone before your next visit to Rome, and send me a selfie of you together. Agreed?'

Angelo was fairly sure he could talk one of

his colleagues into posing for a photograph to make it look as if they were dating. If that would keep his dad happy, it'd be worth asking for a favour. 'Deal.'

'Good.' His father gave him a hug. 'Safe journey. Text me when you're home.'

'Of course I will. Have a good week, Dad.' Angelo hugged him back.

But on the way back to Florence he picked up a message from his boss, Ric Fanelli.

Muswell Hill Memorial Hospital is sending one of their team to us for a three-month secondment in the new unit. She starts Thursday. Can I ask you to help her settle in and translate?

As Angelo was half-English and had trained in London, he wasn't surprised by the request. But then he saw the name of their new doctor.

No.

It couldn't be her.

Surely.

He clicked on the link to her profile on the hospital website, and the photograph took his breath away.

Sam Clarke. Two years older and two years more beautiful.

He'd had no idea that she'd moved into foetal surgery. He hadn't seen her since he'd come back to Italy; their break-up had been by phone, because he hadn't trusted himself to go through with it if he'd looked her in the eye. Though, a year ago—when his dad was stable enough for Angelo to be sure he wasn't leaving Sam open to potential hurt—he'd gone back to London, ready to open his heart to her and apologise for the way he'd left. To tell her the truth about his dad's addiction and the way he was still coming to terms with losing his mum, and ask her to forgive him. He'd turned up at their old department at lunchtime, hoping he might be able to find out when she was off duty. The receptionist was someone he didn't know, so clearly she'd joined the department since he'd left.

'I used to work here,' he said, 'and I wanted to look up some old friends while I'm in London. Would you be able to tell me what shift Sam Clarke is on, please?'

'Oh, Sam's not in today,' the receptionist said. 'She's gone to Liverpool for the weekend with Greg.'

'Greg?' Who was Greg? Another new person in the department?

'Her boyfriend.' The receptionist smiled. 'He's so lovely. Swept her off her feet. I wouldn't be surprised if he pops the question, this weekend.'

What?

Sam was dating someone else, and it was getting serious?

For a moment, he couldn't quite piece it all together, and then the realisation slammed into him.

He'd left it too late.

But, if she was happy, it wouldn't be fair to turn her life upside down again. He'd been miserable for the last year, feeling guilty that he'd missed all the signs with his dad and wishing that his mum had still been around to share his worries and help him work out a plan. What could he really offer Sam, except more of the uncertainty that came with addiction? And what if it was too much for her and she left him anyway?

All the pain and longing would've been for nothing.

So maybe it would be better to do the right thing and go back to Italy without seeing her.

'Do you want to leave a message for her?' the receptionist asked.

'No, you're all right,' he said, forcing a smile he didn't feel. 'Thanks, anyway.' He'd managed to square his shoulders and saunter away as if his heart wasn't breaking into tiny pieces all over again.

And now it looked as if their paths were going to cross again for the next three months.

Had the woman been right and Greg had asked Sam to marry him, that weekend? Were they engaged, or even married?

Sam's profile on the hospital website was focused on professional matters, and they weren't friends on social media, so he had no idea. At least he had a couple of days to get used to the idea of seeing her again. But the prospect of having Sam back in his life, even temporarily, made him feel as if he was hurtling down from the top of a rollercoaster at full speed. Just how was he going to deal with this?

On Wednesday morning, Sam caught the plane to Pisa. When she'd collected her luggage, she checked the notes on her phone: next was the people-mover from the airport to the train station, and then the train to Florence.

She bought the tickets she needed, along with a sandwich and a bottle of water, took the people-mover to the train station, then found her seat on the train to Florence and enjoyed looking out at the scenery. Tuscany was such a pretty part of Italy, with its tall, narrow cypress trees and spreading vineyards; the river Arno ran alongside the train tracks, broadening into beautiful water meadows. Now, in the spring, everywhere was green, feeling fresh and new.

According to the map on her phone, her new flat was easily within walking distance from the station in Florence. And it turned out to be a gorgeous walk: narrow streets with flagstone paving, lined by four-storey buildings in tones of saffron and dark cream with shuttered windows. Everywhere she looked, there were ancient churches and towers; there were statues on corners and in niches, and stunning little details on every bit of ironwork she saw. No wonder Florence was a top destination for art-lovers.

Then she turned a corner and the famous cathedral was right in front of her, with the octagonal Duomo and its red-tiled roof. From photographs, she'd always thought the facade of the building was black and white, but up close she could see tones of dark green and cream and red. It was absolutely stunning. And to think she'd go past this every day on the way to work: how fantastic was that?

Smiling, she headed to the concierge's office to pick up her keys. Her flat was in a sixteenth-century stone building; there was a huge wooden doorway with a lion's head knocker. How many people had used that knocker and walked through that door, over the centuries?

Although there was no lift to the top floor, she didn't mind. Taking the stairs would keep her fit. At the same time, she was glad she'd travelled relatively light and only had the one suitcase to haul up three flights of stairs.

She unlocked the door and left her case by the doorway while she explored inside.

Most of the walls in the living room had been painted white, but Sam was thrilled to see that the top of one wall actually had the remains of an ancient fresco. Compared with her very modern flat in London, this was incredible: a building with art that someone had made five hundred years ago.

There was a comfortable-looking sofa in the living room, with a stripped wooden floor and a rug in rich tones of blue; a small bistro table and two ladderback chairs stood next to an archway that led to a compact kitchen. The kitchen area, too, was decorated in neutral tones, with pale counters and light wood cupboard doors; here, the flooring was terracotta flagstone.

The marble-tiled bathroom had a good-sized shower. The last room was a bedroom, again with stripped wooden flooring and a rug; there was a wrought-iron double bedstead, a gilt-framed mirror and a large ward-robe. The window had wooden shutters; Sam opened them to see the view, and then realised with delight that she could actually see the Duomo above the terracotta rooftops.

She took a snap to send to her mum and her best friend, captioning it.

A room with a view—it doesn't get more amazing than this!

It was still hard to believe that she was going to be living right in the historic centre of a city she'd always wanted to visit, doing a job that she loved.

And she couldn't wait for the next three months to start.

The concierge had given her an envelope along with her keys. She opened it to discover a note written in perfect English from one of her colleagues, welcoming her to Florence. Lidia had left her some milk and fresh coffee in the fridge, a loaf of bread and a bag of delicious-looking cookies in the cupboard, directions to the supermarket and a note of the best places to buy bread, cheese, fruit and vegetables locally, as well as advice about a couple of good places to eat nearby.

Sam made herself a quick coffee to go with

the cookies—which tasted even better than they looked—to restore some of her energy from travelling, then headed out to buy food, plus some flowers to say thank you to Lidia. And she was pleased to discover that her language skills, helped by the app she'd been using for the last few days, were starting to come back; the shopkeepers were more than happy to help remind her of some of the words she'd forgotten.

Words that Angelo had taught her, patiently guiding her initial stumbling efforts and rewarding her with kisses…

She shook herself. That part of her life was over and done with. What was the point of wishing for what might have been? Angelo had made it clear enough that he didn't love her any more. He'd said he needed to go back to Italy to sort out some family stuff, and when she'd asked him what she could do to help he'd mumbled vague excuses. He'd barely answered the supportive texts she'd sent. And then he'd called her, out of the blue.

'Sam, there isn't a good way to say this, so I'm going to be honest with you. Things aren't working out between us.'

She'd been so shocked that she hadn't been able to say a word.

'I'm staying in Italy,' he'd continued.

'But—I thought—' She'd stumbled over the words. They'd been so good together.

'I'm sorry. I realised when I was here, I don't love you the way you deserve to be loved.'

'But—'

'Sorry. Be happy.' And he'd ended the call.

She'd been devastated. Angelo had met her a few months after her brother's death, when she'd been a walking shadow of guilt and misery, convinced that there must've been something she'd missed and she could've saved Dominic. They'd become friends and he'd made her realise that addiction was hard to help and nobody could've done more for her brother. And friendship had turned to love... or so she'd thought.

But Angelo hadn't loved her, after all.

And she didn't have a clue where it had gone wrong. It had taken her months to pick herself up and dust herself down again. Not that she'd made a huge success of it. Even though Greg from the Emergency Department was a lovely guy, she'd realised that she was dating him on the rebound and that wasn't fair, so she'd told him as gently as she could that they needed to go back to being just good friends. She hadn't dated since, burying herself in her work.

But maybe Florence would help her move away from the past. A summer in the Italian sunshine. And when she returned to London, after her secondment, she'd be ready to try again.

On the way back to her flat, Sam walked along the riverbank, enjoying the view of the bridges—and particularly the huge stone arch of the Ponte Vecchio, with its little shops and its perfect reflection in the River Arno. She took another snap to send home, then headed through a courtyard and found herself in front of a huge and very famous statue indeed: Michelangelo's *David*. She knew it was a copy, with the original housed safely in a nearby museum, but it was still a surprise—and a joy—to see famous sights almost everywhere she turned.

She took yet another snap to send home, and then she headed back to her flat. Florence, she thought, was going to be an incredible experience.

The next morning, Sam went for a run before her shift; the artists were just setting up their stalls by the Duomo and getting ready to paint more small watercolours for the tourists, and she could hear the bustle of market stalls being set up nearby. Cafés were starting to open, and she could smell the scents of coffee and freshly baked bread. Late spring flowers were everywhere: climbing up walls, spilling over window boxes and blooming in the large terracotta pots she always associated with Italy. The streets here were cobbled, and somehow the city managed to look completely ancient and thoroughly modern all at the same time.

Endorphins from the run and pleasure from the views set her up for the day, and Sam was still smiling when she walked into the Michelangelo Hospital. At the reception area, she picked up the lanyard with her ID card, and asked for directions to Ricardo Fanelli's office.

When she reached the maternity department and pressed her ID card to the reader, nothing happened; clearly her card hadn't been activated yet. Not wanting to be late on her first day, she pressed the buzzer.

There was an answering buzz, and a few seconds later the door opened.

And her knees buckled for a moment when she saw who'd opened the door to her. She almost dropped the flowers she'd bought to thank Lidia.

It couldn't be Angelo. How could he be working in Florence, when she knew he lived in Rome?

But the name on the lanyard round his neck was very clear: *Dottore Angelo Brunelli*.

The love of her life. The man who'd told her he didn't love her any more.

CHAPTER TWO

'HELLO, SAM,' ANGELO SAID. 'Welcome to the Michelangelo Hospital.' He held out his hand, offering her a formal handshake, as if to prove that they'd both got over the past.

The second her palm touched his, her skin felt as if it was fizzing. Memories bubbled over, of how she'd touched him in the past. Linked her hand with his as they'd walked along, talking. Wrapped her arms round him as they'd danced together. Slid her hands through his hair as he'd kissed her. Stroked his bare skin as they'd made love...

She hadn't been prepared for this. She'd thought she was working in a brand-new unit with Ric Fanelli and Henri Lefevre. She'd been so busy over the last three days, packing and sorting out her flight and accommodation and saying goodbye to everyone, that it hadn't even occurred to her to look up the rest of her new department.

But clearly Angelo had known she was coming here, because there wasn't the slightest trace of surprise in his expression.

'I didn't realise you worked here,' she said, forcing herself to sound calm and collected—even though seeing him again had sent her into a spin. 'I thought you were in Rome.'

He inclined his head. 'I moved here a year ago.'

And he looked just the same as she remembered. The same unruly hair that he tried to keep neat for work, but it insisted on curling and tended to stick out everywhere by the end of a shift. The same dark, soulful eyes with their incredibly long lashes. The same beautiful mouth that had made her heart feel as if it had done a triple somersault whenever he smiled at her.

She glanced at her watch, affecting a coolness she most definitely didn't feel. 'I'm meant to be meeting Professor Fanelli and Professor Lefevre,' she said. 'If you could perhaps point me in the right direction—and also tell me first where I can find Lidia—that would be appreciated.'

'Of course,' he said. 'Actually, Ric asked me to help you settle in and translate for you.'

She went cold. Oh, no. Please don't let everyone in Florence know that Angelo was her ex. This would be beyond awkward.

'On the grounds,' he continued, 'that I'm half-English and trained in London.'

She almost sagged in relief as she realised he was telling her that nobody knew about their shared past. That he was going to pretend they were strangers. 'That would be kind.' It wasn't how she felt about it at all, but she needed to keep things professional.

'I'll take you to Lidia,' he said, and ushered her down the corridor.

Lidia turned out to be one of the midwives, half-Italian and half-Jamaican, with a broad smile and kind eyes.

'I just wanted to say thank you,' Sam said when Angelo had introduced them, 'for settling me in to the flat. I really appreciated being able to make myself a coffee when I got in. Those cookies were utterly delicious.'

'No problem, *cara*,' Lidia said. 'And these flowers are gorgeous. Thank you.' She smiled. 'If you're free for lunch and I'm not with a mum, come and find me.'

'I'll do that,' Sam said.

Angelo made no comment, but took her down to Ricardo Fanelli's office, rapped on the door and opened it at the call of, *'Avanti!'*

'Dr Clarke's here,' he said, and gestured to

her to go inside. 'Welcome again to the department, Dr Clarke. Enjoy your first morning.'

'Wait, Angelo—you might as well stay,' Ricardo said as Angelo turned away, 'because Dr Clarke will be working with you.'

Sam really hoped that the dismay didn't show on her face. She still hadn't come to terms with the idea of Angelo working in the same city as her, let alone working closely with him.

'Pia Bianchi—the mum with triplets and twin-to-twin transfusion syndrome,' Ricardo said, 'is on Angelo's list. But let me introduce everyone, first. Professor Henri Lefevre,' he gestured to the man seated beside him, 'meet Dr Samantha Clarke and Dr Angelo Brunelli.'

There were smiles and handshakes all round.

'I prefer to work on first name terms,' Ricardo said, 'so please call me Ric. May I ask, Samantha, how much Italian do you speak?'

'Please, do call me Sam. I've been trying to brush up my Italian since my boss asked me to join you, but it's still a bit rusty,' she said, not daring to look at Angelo, who'd taught her nearly all of the Italian she knew, 'and I'm afraid my vocabulary's much more social than medical.'

'You'll be surprised by how quickly you get

a language back,' Ric said with a smile. 'And you'll soon pick up the medical side; in the meantime, Angelo can help translate for you. He's half English and trained in England.'

Yeah. She knew that already: his mum had been an English GP and fallen in love with his dad while on holiday in Rome. She'd met the English side of Angelo's family and liked them very much. Not that she could say so without things getting really awkward.

'Of course,' Angelo said, sounding very professional. No doubt this was going to be as difficult for him as it was for her. And, as the head of department had clearly decided that they were working together, Sam knew she and Angelo were going to need a chat to clear the air.

Thankfully the meeting itself was relatively brief, more of a welcome and an explanation of everyone's roles. Ric was working on strategy, Henri was overseeing the surgical team, and Sam was treating patients and training staff—starting with Angelo.

A quarter of an hour later, Angelo said, 'We need to get going, Ric. Pia Bianchi is having a scan right now. I want to review the scan before her appointment, and I also need to brief Dr Clarke on the situation.'

Ric said, 'If you and Angelo decide on surgery for the triplets, Sam, then it would be a good teaching case.'

'Agreed,' Sam said. 'Provided they give me permission, of course.'

'Of course. See the Bianchis, then Angelo can show you round the department and introduce you to everyone,' Ric said with a smile. 'I'll catch up with you later.'

So it was official that they'd be working together. At some point they were going to have to talk about the past. Quite how they were going to do that, she wasn't sure. For now, she'd stick to talking about work.

She followed Angelo to the consulting room in silence. He didn't speak as he logged into the computer and brought up the scan file, but she could see from his expression that it wasn't great news.

'Right. Pia and Tommaso Bianchi,' he said. 'Pia's thirty-six. It's her first pregnancy. She had problems conceiving and was diagnosed with PCOS. The third round of IVF was successful, and she's twenty-two weeks pregnant with twins and a singleton.'

The brief patient history hid what sounded like months and months of worry, and Sam's heart went out to Pia.

'Throughout the pregnancy, she's been well. Obviously, because triplet pregnancies are more complicated than singletons, we've been monitoring her fortnightly since sixteen weeks,' he said. 'Last week, I suspected the beginning of TTTS. I wasn't happy with Monday's scan because there was a noticeable difference between the twins—they were at stage two—and I'm even less happy with this morning's scan, because I think we're at borderline stage three.' He twisted the monitor round so she could see the two scans side by side. The second scan definitely showed a difference; they clearly needed to step in rather than watch and wait.

'Agreed,' Sam said. 'What's her delivery plan?'

'Originally it was for a managed delivery at thirty-five weeks—' which Sam knew was standard for an uncomplicated triplet pregnancy '—but, now TTTS is involved, I want to revise that to thirty-three weeks.' He grimaced. 'To be frank, I think anything after thirty weeks would be a bonus, and I'm planning to give her steroid injections at twenty-nine weeks.'

To mature the babies' lungs in case they needed an emergency delivery; it was a sensible plan, Sam thought.

'Would I be right in thinking that the twins are MCDA?' she asked. Monochorionic diamniotic twins—meaning they shared a single placenta with a single outer membrane, but two inner membranes—were the type at highest risk of developing TTTS.

'Yes.' He gestured to the screen. 'So what do you think?'

'My gut feel is we need to do laser surgery rather than amnioreduction—and I think my boss had the same view or he wouldn't have sent me out here,' she said. 'But we need to give the parents all the options and let them make an informed decision. We can give guidance, but at the end of the day it's their choice and our job is to support them.'

'Agreed,' he said.

She was relieved that Angelo's attitude towards parents was the same as it had been when they'd last worked together: that their views were important, and his job as a doctor was to give them all the information to help them make the right decision for their situation and then support them. At least she wouldn't have to fight him on that score.

'Is there anything else you need to know before I call the Bianchis in?' he asked.

'No, you've covered everything.'

After getting the parents settled, he introduced Sam as the new surgeon on their team.

'I trained in England,' she said, in careful

Italian, 'and I'm here because I work with babies inside the womb.'

'We can speak in English, if you prefer,' Tommaso said.

'That's very kind, but it's not fair to you to have to think in a different language when you're already worried,' she said with a smile. 'I'll do my best to be clear in Italian.'

'And I'll help with any translation issues,' Angelo added.

She smiled her thanks at him.

'Signor and Signora Bianchi, I see that you've already had an ultrasound, a foetal MRI and an echocardiography of the babies' hearts today,' Sam said, glancing at Angelo to check she'd got the terms right and relieved to see his nod. 'I'm sure Dr Brunelli—Angelo—has already explained about twin-to-twin transfusion syndrome to you, but I'd like to be sure you have all the information you need to make a decision on how you want us to help you, so forgive me if any of this is repeating things for you. The condition is to do with the placenta rather than the baby, and it's absolutely not your fault. It happens in around one in seven twin pregnancies, and we don't actually know why it happens. What we do know is that the babies share some of the blood vessels in the placenta, so the blood flow between them isn't equal.'

She drew a quick diagram on the whiteboard. 'So we have your three babies: one with his own placenta, and the twins sharing another placenta. The one on his own isn't affected. But the connection between the blood vessels on the twins' placenta means that blood is transferred from the donor—let's call him twin one—to the recipient. Let's call him twin two.' She circled the first twin. 'Twin one doesn't have as much blood flow as he should, and the body prioritises blood flow to the brain so his kidneys aren't getting enough blood. He's dehydrated, he isn't growing as much as he should, he isn't producing as much urine as he should, and he doesn't have as much amniotic fluid around him as he should.'

She paused to check that the Bianchis were following. At their nod, she circled the second twin on the whiteboard and continued, 'Twin two is the other way round: he's getting too much blood and producing more urine than he should. His bladder will become enlarged, he's got too much amniotic fluid, and his heart has to pump harder so the condition will put a strain on his heart.'

'Are they going to die?'

Pia Bianchi was biting her lip, and Sam reached over to squeeze her hand. 'We're here to help, and we want your babies to arrive safely,' she said gently. 'Dr Brunelli and I have discussed your situation, and there are three choices. They're your babies, so how you both feel about the options is important. But we want you to know exactly what everything entails, so you can make an informed decision.'

The Bianchis both looked relieved.

'The first option is that we just wait and see,' Sam said.

'But we wouldn't really recommend that,' Angelo said. 'We've looked at the scans, and you can see the difference in size between twin one and twin two even since Monday.' He showed the screen to the Bianchis. 'And I can see your bump's a lot bigger than when I saw you on Monday, Pia.'

'It feels as if I'm nine months pregnant, not five and a half,' Pia admitted. 'It's not very comfortable. I did wonder if it was because I'm carrying triplets.'

'No. It's the twin-to-twin transfusion causing that. If we wait and do nothing,' Sam said gently, 'then I'm sorry to say I think it's very likely you'll lose both twins, and in turn that's likely to trigger the miscarriage of your third baby.'

'You're a surgeon, Dr Clarke—does that mean Pia needs to have surgery?' Tommaso asked.

'In my view, yes. And there are two things we can do to help the babies,' Sam said. 'The first one is that I can drain the excess amniotic fluid from twin two, which should help, and we'll do another scan in a couple of days to see how you're all doing. If draining the fluid has worked, then we can go back to weekly monitoring. Though I should warn you that draining the fluid doesn't correct the problem with the blood vessels that causes the excess fluid in the first place, so we might have to repeat the operation.'

'What if draining the fluid doesn't work?' Pia asked.

'Then we have a second option: laser surgery,' Sam explained. 'That's where I'd seal off the blood vessel connections that aren't working properly in the placenta, and then I'd drain the excess fluid. You'd need to stay in hospital for a day after the surgery, and we'd reassess the babies again before you go home.'

'Or you can go straight to laser surgery without trying to drain the excess amniotic fluid first,' Angelo added.

'Surgery.' Pia was white-faced. 'Will our babies survive?'

'We'll be honest with you,' Angelo said.

Strictly speaking, the Bianchis were on his list rather than hers, so Sam understood that Angelo wanted to be the one to answer the question—just as she would, in his shoes. At the same time, she appreciated the 'we', because he was including her and making it clear they were a team. They might be poles apart in their personal life but at least here they were on the same side.

'There's always a risk with surgery, and this is an invasive procedure so, yes, there is a risk of miscarriage,' Angelo said. 'At the moment, that'd be a ten per cent chance of miscarrying.'

'Ten per cent's an awful lot,' Pia said, looking horrified.

'If you look at it the other way round, there's also a ninety per cent chance that at least one of the twins will survive,' Sam said. 'The risk of miscarriage decreases after you reach twenty-four weeks, plus we'll keep a very close eye on you.'

'What are the chances that both of the twins will survive, if you do the surgery?' Tommaso asked.

'The chances for both of them are slightly lower than they are for just one of them,' Sam said. 'As Angelo said, with all surgery there's a risk. But the chances of them both being fine is much higher than the risk of losing both of them.'

'Could we wait to do the operation until I'm twenty-four weeks, when the risk of miscarriage is lower?' Pia asked.

'Given the changes in the scan since Monday, I really wouldn't want to risk waiting another two weeks,' Angelo said. 'But, whatever you choose to do, please be reassured that we'll keep a very close eye on you and we'll support you. If you're concerned at any point, then we want you to call us rather than staying at home and worrying.'

'There are three babies,' Tommaso said. 'If we have the surgery on the twins, will the other baby be safe even if—if one of the twins doesn't make it?'

'I've worked with triplet pregnancies involving twin-to-twin syndrome in London,' Sam reassured him, 'and I'm pleased to tell you I delivered all the babies safely in every case. As we've said, there's always a risk with surgery, but the odds are in your favour.'

'What would you do if they were your babies?' Tommaso asked. 'Take away the fluid or have the surgery?'

'If I'm honest, the option I'd prefer—both as a doctor, and if I was in your shoes—is laser surgery,' Sam said.

The Bianchis looked at Angelo.

'The same goes for me,' he said quietly. 'I believe it will give the babies the best chance.'

'How does the laser surgery work?' Pia asked.

'Your scan shows me the placenta is on the back wall of your uterus, so you'll have a local anaesthetic and sedation. That means you'll be awake for the procedure, but you won't feel any pain,' Sam explained. 'I'll make a small incision in your tummy and put a metal tube into your uterus.'

'A metal tube?' Tommaso's eyes widened.

'It's much thinner than you're probably thinking,' she reassured him. 'Thinner than a drinking straw. I promise you, it's not going to hurt Pia. Then I'll put a special kind of camera—called a fetoscope—through the tube to let me see all the blood vessel connections on the surface of the twins' placenta.'

'The camera's that small?' Tommaso asked, looking surprised.

'Yes. It's fibre optic,' Sam said. 'Through the camera lens, I'll be able to see which blood vessels aren't working properly, and I'll put a laser down the tube and use the laser to seal those blood vessels and disconnect them. That means the blood will be flowing normally again to both twins. Finally, I'll drain the excess amniotic fluid, which will make you feel a lot more comfortable, too.'

Pia looked thoughtful. 'If you have to operate on the placenta, does that mean I can't have a vaginal delivery?'

'That's entirely up to you,' Sam said. 'I'll sever all the blood vessels that shouldn't be joined, so it'll be safe to deliver vaginally. But if you decide you'd rather have a Caesarean section, that's also fine.'

'Because there's been a complication during your pregnancy, we'll want you to deliver the triplets a bit earlier than we originally planned,' Angelo said.

'How soon?' Tommaso asked.

'We'd aim for thirty-three weeks, but I'll be honest and tell you that anything after thirty weeks will be a bonus. They'll be tiny at thirty weeks, and they'll need special care, but they'll be old enough to cope with life outside the womb,' Sam said. 'We'll need to give you an injection of steroids at twenty-nine weeks to mature their lungs, Pia, just to be on the safe side. But it's very likely that the babies will need to be in the special care baby unit for a while after they're born.'

'We can't say how long they'll be in the special care unit—it depends on how the babies respond. But we can arrange for you to have a tour of the unit before the babies arrive,' Angelo added, 'so you'll know what to expect and it'll make the unit feel much less scary.'

'Don't panic, and don't think you have to make a decision this very second,' Sam said. 'You've got time to go away and talk it over with your family and friends. Right now the twin-to-twin syndrome is borderline stage two to three, so I don't have to whisk you straight into theatre. If you want to go ahead, we can do the fluid reduction or the laser surgery tomorrow.'

'What I would advise is don't look up complicated birth stories on the internet,' Angelo said. 'You'll find too many stories that will worry you.'

'I can print you a leaflet that explains the procedures, so you don't have to try to remember it,' Sam said. She glanced at Angelo, who nodded.

'I'll do that now,' he said, and tapped a couple of keys on his computer.

'It's a lot to take in. I'd advise you to go and sit somewhere pretty so you can think about it,' Sam said. 'Have a drink and something to eat. Talk to the people you love, write down all your questions, and come back and see us this afternoon so we can work through every single question and be sure you're happy to make a decision.' She shook their hands. 'The main thing is—and I know it's a lot easier to say than do—try not to worry. We're here. And we'll support you, whatever you decide to do.'

'If you'd like to come with me,' Angelo said, 'we can pick up that leaflet from the reception desk.'

'And we'll see you this afternoon,' Sam said.

Sam had always been kind, Angelo remembered. And the Bianchis had definitely reacted to her warmth.

She sat in with the rest of his clinic, that morning; most of his cases were straightforward, though there was another set of twins that they'd need to keep an eye on. At the end of the clinic, Angelo took her round the department to introduce her to as many of the other staff as he could find. Then he glanced at his watch. 'We've got half an hour for a lunch break.'

'I was going to lunch with Lidia, if she's not in with a mum,' she said.

'Let me check for you.' Angelo made a brief enquiry, then shook his head. 'She's in the delivery suite. Why don't I show you where the canteen is and buy you lunch?'

'Thank you,' she said politely. 'That's kind of you to show me round, but I'd prefer to buy my own lunch.'

Sam had always been independent, he remembered. Plus he couldn't ignore the way things had ended between them: he knew he'd hurt her badly. Of course a sandwich and coffee wasn't even going to begin to make up for that, and she wouldn't want to accept anything from him. In her shoes, he'd feel the same. Though he wasn't quite sure how to broach the subject. Or how to apologise in a way that she'd know he really meant it—other than by telling her the truth. And that would be tricky. He didn't want to hurt her even more.

'I know you'd probably rather not spend time with me,' he said, 'but we need to clear the air a bit, since we'll be working together.'

'Agreed,' she said.

How did you apologise for breaking someone's heart?

He couldn't help glancing at her left hand. There was no ring, but that didn't mean anything. She was a surgeon, and hygiene regulations meant wearing no jewellery. Had she ended up marrying the guy she'd been dating a year ago? Her name was the same, though she might've decided not to change it after marriage. But how could he ask without it seeming crass? It was none of his business.

She still looked the same as she had two years ago, except she'd had her blonde hair cut short, in a choppy pixie cut that suited her. Still had the same cool grey eyes, the same beautiful rosebud mouth—a mouth he'd kissed until it made him dizzy. Seeing her made him feel dizzy now, and there was nothing he could do about it. Though at least she'd agreed to talk to him. That was a start.

In the canteen, he bought himself a sandwich and coffee, waited for her to do the same, and found a quiet table.

'It looks as if we're going to be working together for the next three months,' he said. 'And I know we're both professional enough to put our patients first. But I know that what I did…' God, this made him feel like a teenage boy, without the social skills to deal with an awkward situation. 'What I'm trying to say,' he said, 'is that I don't want things to be difficult between us at work. And I owe you an apology.' What he really owed her was an explanation, but it was a messy and complicated story—and the staff canteen most definitely wasn't the right place to tell it.

She shrugged. 'It was a long time ago. We're both older and wiser.'

'For the record, Sam, I'm truly sorry I hurt you,' he said quietly.

For a moment, he thought he saw the sheen of tears in her eyes. There was a time when he could've reached across the table and squeezed her hand. A time when he could've wrapped her in his arms and told her everything was going to work out just fine. But he'd forfeited that right when he'd walked out on her.

But then she blinked. 'I really wasn't expecting to see you here. I thought you lived in Rome.'

'I did.' Though she didn't need to know about the year he'd taken off work to look after his dad. 'I was offered a position here, a year ago. The Michelangelo is a good place to work, and Florence is a lovely place to live.' He paused. He already knew the answer to this, but he needed to find some way of making conversation before this got too awkward. 'So you're here for three months?'

She nodded. 'I'm helping to set up the new unit with Professor Lefevre, and doing some of the training. I gather from Ric that I'll be training you, so if the Bianchis opt for laser surgery and give their permission, maybe you can do some of the ablation.'

'Thank you. I'd like that,' Angelo said. 'What made you specialise in foetal medicine?'

'I went to a series of lectures at the London Victoria,' she said. 'And it just fascinated me: the fact that you could make such a difference to the outcome of a pregnancy and treat a baby inside the womb. I talked to my boss about it and asked if I could do some work in the area. He agreed, and I've gradually specialised. I moved to Muswell Hill a year ago, and I'm looking forward to working with the team here.' She looked at him. 'And you've stayed with general obstetrics rather than specialising?'

'Yes.' Just not in the hospital, the city or even the country where he'd originally planned to work. 'The team here's really nice.'

'Good to know.'

Reduced to small talk, after all they'd shared. This felt like nails raking down a blackboard. But Angelo knew it was his own fault. Two years ago, he'd believed he was protecting Sam by walking away instead of involving her and bringing back all the memories of her brother's struggle with addiction and eventual death. He'd thought he was protecting himself, too— that if he was the one to end it, he wouldn't be so badly hurt. What he'd actually done was to make the biggest mistake of his life. He should've been honest with her about his dad's situation and given her the choice, instead of making the decision for her. At the time, he'd thought he was being noble and doing the right thing. Now, he was beginning to think that maybe he'd just been arrogant. Either way, he'd been stupid. And he shouldn't have left it a whole year before going back for her.

Seeing her again had stirred up all the old feelings, and it had also made him understand exactly why all his relationships had fizzled out since he'd been back in Italy: because nobody had ever matched up to Sam.

Somehow he managed to keep talking to her about trivial things—good places to eat in the city, must-see attractions and the best times to avoid the crowds—and then it was time to go back for afternoon clinic.

They saw three more sets of parents before the Bianchis came back in.

'We've looked up the websites you recommended, made notes and talked it over with our families,' Pia said. 'And we've decided.' She and Tommaso shared a glance. 'We want to do the laser therapy because we think it'll give the twins their best chance.'

'Then I'll slot you in for first thing tomorrow morning,' Sam said. 'I know you've made your decision, but do you have any questions for us?'

Pia nodded. 'You did say to write them down.'

'Absolutely. That way, you can make sure you've asked everything, instead of getting nearly home and remembering something you forgot to ask,' Sam said with a smile.

Pia brought out her phone and opened a list.

Sam dealt with each question calmly and patiently, and Angelo was pleased to see that the Bianchis both looked a lot less tense by the end.

Sam gave them a quick reminder of what they needed to do before the operation, then smiled. 'So tomorrow afternoon you're going to feel a lot more comfortable, Pia—and you'll both be a lot less worried about the babies.'

'We've been a bit frantic, ever since the last couple of scans,' Tommaso admitted.

'We'll do our best to keep your babies safe,' Sam promised him. 'I do have a couple of questions for you, if that's all right?'

'Sure,' Tommaso said.

'Angelo and I will be in Theatre with you tomorrow, along with a couple of midwives, one of the neonatal team and the anaesthetist, which is pretty much standard. Would you mind if we had three or four other people in the team observing the procedure?' Sam asked. 'Obviously there's no pressure to say yes. I completely understand if you'd rather not.'

'But, if you don't mind Sam using the procedure to teach others,' Angelo said, 'it means you'd be under even closer supervision.'

'And, if you don't mind, I'd like Angelo to do some of the lasering—which will be under my close supervision and instruction,' Sam said. 'Again, please don't feel that you have to say yes. We'll completely understand if you'd rather not, and it won't make any difference to the way we treat you. Our main aim is to support you, and I want you to be comfortable.'

The Bianchis exchanged a glance. 'No, that's all fine,' Pia said. 'You've been very open with us. Kind. We trust you.'

Once they'd finished clinic, Sam turned to Angelo. 'I know you've got ward rounds now, but I'd like to catch Ric and Henri and tell them about tomorrow's op,' she said.

'Of course. Do you need me to show you again where Ric's room is?'

'It's fine. I'll find it,' she said. 'And thank you. I know this isn't easy for you.'

'It isn't easy for either of us,' he said.

'No.' She took a deep breath. 'I appreciate you being so accommodating.'

That was one way of putting it, Angelo thought. But what other choice did he have?

Three months, and she'd be out of his life again.

He could work with her for three months. Just keep it cool, calm and professional. And put a lid on the feelings that threatened to spill out.

CHAPTER THREE

'SO HOW WAS your first day?' Nina, Sam's best friend, asked down the phone.

'Good,' Sam said with a smile, curling up on her sofa.

'Are your colleagues nice?'

'Yes. Ric Fanelli's a sweetie, and although Henri Lefevre's a tiny bit scary I think he'll be nice when I get to know him.' She took a deep breath. 'But, um, I did have a bit of a surprise today.' Which was the understatement of the year. 'Angelo works here.'

'What, *your* Angelo?' Nina sounded shocked.

'He hasn't been mine for two years,' Sam reminded her dryly. 'But, yes, Angelo Brunelli.'

'Ouch. That's going to be awkward. He's not on your team, is he?' Nina asked.

'You know that twin-to-twin transfusion syndrome case Will told me about, the one they brought me over to treat? The mum happens to be on Angelo's list—so, yes, I'm working with him. We're doing some laser ablation together tomorrow.'

Nina sucked in a breath. 'Oh, that's tough. Are you going to be OK?'

'I'll have to be, if I want to be part of this project,' Sam said. 'Which I do.'

'It's still awkward.' Nina paused. 'Has he changed?'

Sam had no idea. 'He looks exactly like he did in London,' she said carefully.

'Like a Raphael cherub, with that messy hair. He always was cute,' Nina said. 'And I really liked him—before he dumped you by phone.'

'It was all a long time ago,' Sam said. Though it still stung. Why hadn't he had the guts to call it off face to face, before he went to Italy?

'So is he married now? Does he have kids?'

'I don't know. We stuck to small talk and patients only,' Sam said. 'For what it's worth, he did apologise for hurting me.'

Nina coughed. 'That's a bit late. And he more than hurt you, Sam. He broke your heart.'

And Sam had never been quite able to move on, even though she'd dated. She'd liked Greg very much, but when he'd wanted to move their relationship to something more serious she'd realised that she wasn't ready. They'd stayed friends, but she'd concentrated on her career rather than her love life ever since. 'It is what it is,' Sam said. 'On the plus side, Florence is even more gorgeous than the photographs. I'm going to start exploring the city properly at the weekend. Everywhere you look is beautiful.'

'Sounds amazing. Send me lots of pics,' Nina said.

They chatted for a bit longer, and then Sam heard a wail. 'It sounds as if Lily's just woken up.'

'Yup. And that's definitely a "hungry" cry,' Nina said.

'I'll let you go. Give my goddaughter a cuddle for me,' Sam said. 'Talk to you soon.'

Part of her felt wistful as she ended the call. She'd hoped that she and Nina would end up having babies around the same time, and their children would grow up being close, though it hadn't worked out that way. But at least her best friend was happy, and Sam enjoyed being close to her goddaughter. To brush the gloominess away, she headed out for a walk along the river, enjoying the bustle of the early evening in the city.

But Nina's question had made her wonder.

Had Angelo moved on? Was he with someone else, now? And, if so, was it serious?

She tried looking him up on a couple of social media sites, but his settings were locked so that only his friends could see whatever he posted and she was left none the wiser. She could hardly ask at work, without stirring up gossip.

Maybe she'd find a way of broaching the subject tactfully tomorrow.

On Friday morning, Sam went for a run to clear her head before breakfast, had a shower, grabbed a coffee and a warm pastry at the small café round the corner from her flat, and walked to the hospital.

Today would be a big day—both for the Bianchis and for the new unit. Along with the team who'd be there as part of the operation, two professors, the senior midwife, two junior doctors and another from the neonatal team would be watching the procedure, and Angelo would be there to assist her with the operation and translate any questions or answers where her language skills fell short.

She'd practised her new vocabulary all evening, wanting to show everyone in the department that she was trying to make an effort to be part of the team and work with them in their own language, rather than expecting everyone to accommodate her by speaking in English. But her own nervousness would be relatively minor compared to the way the Bianchis would be feeling, she knew. She went to see them before they were due to see the anaesthetist, just to reassure them and answer any last-minute questions.

Angelo was already there. He looked up and smiled as she walked in, and it made her heart feel as if it had done a backflip.

Not here, and not now, she reminded herself. She and Angelo had stopped being a couple two years ago. And, even if he turned out to be single, she wasn't giving him the chance to walk out on her again.

'Are you ready?' she asked Pia.

'I think so.' Pia swallowed hard. 'Actually, no. I'm scared.'

'Anyone would be, in your shoes. But, I promise you, I've done this before. You might feel a little bit of discomfort at times, but it won't be painful and it won't hurt the babies.' Sam squeezed her hand in reassurance. 'Try not to worry. The nice thing is that you'll actually get a proper look at your babies in the womb today. So you've got something to look forward to. Hold on to that instead of the worry.'

'Thank you,' Pia whispered.

The anaesthetist came in and Angelo introduced her to everyone.

'Time for Angelo and me to go and scrub up. We'll see you in Theatre,' Sam said with a smile.

Even though Sam's presence stirred up all kinds of feelings that Angelo would rather keep stuffed in their box, he was looking forward to the operation, intrigued to see how she'd handle it.

She chatted to him as they scrubbed up, treating him the same as she did all her other new colleagues, then talked him through exactly what was going to happen with the laser and what she'd need him to do. 'If you need me to go through any of that again,' she said, 'that's fine. I'm happy to repeat myself a dozen times, as long as you're comfortable with what you're going to do.'

'You made it very clear,' he said. 'Though if I can do the ablation for two of the blood vessels—one where you talk me through it step by step, and one where I talk you through what I'm going to do just before I do it and you stop me if I've got anything wrong—I think that would be useful.'

'That's fine,' she said. 'See how you go. It

depends how many blood vessels there are; you might get the chance to do more than two.'

When they'd worked together before, they'd been equals. Now Sam was his senior; plus she was teaching him a new procedure. Though, in a way, it reminded Angelo of when he'd first started to teach her Italian, correcting her pronunciation and encouraging her to broaden her vocabulary. She'd been a good student, methodical and consistent, and he had a feeling that she would be just as good as a teacher.

Though she wouldn't be rewarding him the way he'd rewarded her, with kisses...

He shook himself. Letting the memories flood in really wasn't going to help. They were colleagues. End of.

When the rest of the team was assembled in Theatre, she introduced herself to them and ran through the operation; she was patient with questions, answering them as clearly as she could.

Then Pia was wheeled in, Tommaso by her side and holding her hand, and the anaesthetist on the other side.

Sam introduced them swiftly to everyone.

'Now, you can change your mind if you want to,' she said gently to Pia, 'and I'll ask everyone to go away. But if you're happy for them to stay it'll mean you'll get to meet more of the team, and also you'll have the chance to ask them any questions you like.'

'I just want it over with, so my babies are safe,' Pia said. 'I really don't mind your colleagues being here.'

'Great. Let's get started. Now, even with the anaesthetic, you'll feel a little bit of pushing, Pia. As I said to you earlier, it might feel a little bit uncomfortable, but it shouldn't hurt. If you're worried about anything, just say and we can stop. We've got all the time in the world,' Sam reassured her.

Angelo reached over to squeeze Pia's free hand. 'Sam's going to be concentrating on the surgery, so talk to me first and I'll do my best to answer any questions. I'll tell Sam if you need her to stop for any reason, OK?'

'Thank you,' Pia said.

'I'm going to talk through everything I do, as I do it,' Sam said, addressing Pia and the team. 'Pia's placenta is on the back wall of the uterus, so we're using a local anaesthetic and sedation. I'm going to make a small incision in her abdomen and then put a metal tube into her uterus to support the instruments I'm using.'

Angelo watched, fascinated by how deft Sam's movements were.

'And now I'm putting the fetoscope in—

that's the telescopic camera, Pia.' She slid the instrument down the tube. 'And here we can see the babies.' She indicated the screen. 'Feet, legs—ah, this is what I wanted. Faces. Just as I promised. So now you get to see your babies properly, Pia and Tommaso.' She smiled. 'Meet your twins.'

'This is incredible,' Pia said, staring at the screen.

'Our babies.' Tommaso's voice was filled with awe. 'Twenty-two weeks old, and we can actually see their faces inside your womb, Pia.'

'I just wish it was for…' Pia bit back a sob.

'For a different reason. I know,' Angelo said, squeezing her hand. 'But we're doing the best we can for all of you.'

'Now, I'm going to take a closer look at the placenta,' Sam said. The screen was filled with shades of blue and red and purple; the veins were very evident. 'You can see the first connection that shouldn't be here,' she added to the team. 'I'm going to look all the way along, so we can see all the blood vessel connections before I seal them. We'll take our time and do this thoroughly.'

She was cool, calm and competent, and Angelo could feel Pia relaxing as Sam talked her way through the procedure.

'Next, it's the laser,' Sam said. 'I'm going

to use it to seal the blood vessels and disconnect them, so their circulations are separate
and blood flows normally again to both twins.
You won't feel anything happening, Pia. I'm
shining the laser through the tube, and in a
second you'll hear a pop as we break the connection and seal the blood vessel. But don't
worry about anything happening to the babies,
because the blood will clot immediately. All
we're doing is separating their blood circula-
tion so they'll each have the right amount of
blood. This won't hurt them.'

The pop when she fired the laser was louder
than Angelo had expected, sounding like a
light switch turning on.

She did two more blood vessels, then turned
to him. 'Angelo?'

She talked him through the first one; her in-
structions were clear and easy to follow.

And then it was his turn to talk through
what he planned to do, doing each step once
she'd given the go-ahead.

Part of him was terrified; one wrong move,
and it could be catastrophic. On the other
hand, part of him was thrilled to bits. He was
helping to perform an operation that would
give the twins the best chance of life—an operation that wouldn't even have been possible
when he'd first started training. This was the

cutting edge of medicine, and he could really understand why Sam loved it. It felt like having his own personal magic wand.

Sam encouraged him to do two more blood vessels, then took over again to finish sealing the last few connections.

'And now I'm going to drain the excess amniotic fluid, Pia, which will make you feel a lot more comfortable,' she said.

Once Sam had finished the procedure, Pia was wheeled out to the recovery area to rest, they scrubbed out, and Sam debriefed the team and answered questions.

Angelo was there to support with the translation, but she'd clearly remembered more than she realised because she didn't need to turn to him for help. He still couldn't help remembering when he'd taught her how to speak his language: the smile in her eyes when she'd said, '*Te amo*, Angelo.'

He'd loved her, too.

So very much.

He'd planned to take her to Rome, that summer, to meet the Italian side of his family—she'd already met his mum's side, in England, and they'd all adored her. And, more importantly, he'd planned to take her to the garden of oranges at the top of the Aventine Hill and ask her to marry him…

Then he realised that Sam was looking at him—and so was everyone else. Clearly she was stuck on the vocabulary she needed to answer a question; lost in his memories, he hadn't been paying attention. 'Sorry,' he said, thinking on his feet. 'I'm still a bit stunned about what we just did. If someone had told me when I was a student that one day I'd get to do *in utero* surgery with a laser, I would never have believed them. And, best of all, it means these babies have a much better chance in a complicated pregnancy.' He smiled. 'Sorry. Can we have the question again?'

Thankfully, he was able to help Sam with the answer. But he really needed to stop dreaming. He had no idea if she was in a relationship, and he probably didn't have the right to know. They had a job to do, and then she was going to leave. Maybe he and Sam could become friends again, but it was clear that would be the limit. He'd hurt her so badly.

And he needed to focus on his job.

All the same, he couldn't help suggesting that they grab a coffee in the staff kitchen, when everyone else had gone back to their own clinics and offices.

'That was amazing,' he said. 'I totally get why you fell in love—' Oh, no. Seriously bad choice of phrase. 'With that kind of surgery,' he added swiftly.

There was a faint stain of colour in her cheeks. 'I like the precision. The fact you can make such a huge difference with such tiny, tiny instruments.'

'And it was good working with you again,' he said, before he could stop himself.

The colour in her cheeks deepened. 'We always did work well together.'

Personally as well as professionally. Yeah. They'd *fitted*.

And he could still remember how it felt to hold her close. Her warmth. Her shape. Her scent. All he'd have to do would be to take one step forward and slide his arms round her…

…and she'd run a mile.

Though something about the way she wouldn't quite meet his eyes made him curious: did she, too, wonder how it would feel to hold him again, feel his arms wrapped round her?

'I, um, need to get on with the paperwork,' she said, sounding a little flustered—unless it was his imagination working overtime and he was hearing what he wanted to hear. 'See you with the Bianchis in a couple of hours,' she added, and left the kitchen.

Had his thoughts shown on his face, and that was what had made her practically bolt from the room? Or had it been her own wayward thoughts driving her?

Angelo shook himself. He needed to get a grip. Keep things professional. And stop dreaming about the might-have-beens.

'How are you doing, Pia?' Sam asked.

'OK. I think.' Pia's face was lined with anxiety. 'I was hoping I'd feel the twins move a bit more by now. I mean, there are three babies, and I'm twenty-two weeks…'

'Even though there's less space in your womb, with triplets,' Sam said, 'you still won't feel them move any earlier than if you were carrying just one baby—and in a first pregnancy that's usually around twenty weeks. It's still really early days. Try not to worry.'

Pia's face said it all for her.

'It's a lot easier said than done,' Sam said ruefully. 'Let's go for a scan and see how the babies are doing. I think you could both do with the reassurance.'

'It's hard,' Tommaso said, 'not being able to do anything to help.'

'I'd say you're doing the best thing possible to help,' Angelo reassured him, 'because you're here and Pia knows she isn't on her own.'

In the ultrasound suite, Angelo rubbed the

gel over Pia's stomach, and Sam stroked the head of the transceiver across Pia's bump.

Had the surgery worked? he wondered. Or were the Bianchis going to have their hearts broken today?

Sam looked at the screen—which she'd turned away from the parents, in case she needed to prepare them for bad news, and Angelo noticed that the sound was off, too. For Pia and Tommaso's sake, he really hoped that this would be good news. The longer Sam looked at the screen, the more the muscles in his back tightened with worry. Had the babies survived the operation? Was Sam going to confirm Pia's worst fears?

But then she smiled and flicked a switch. 'Listen to this. This is twin one's heartbeat.' The sound was steady and regular. 'Twin two.' Again, the heartbeat was steady. 'And baby three.'

A single tear leaked down Pia's face. 'They're still alive. All of them. They're still *alive*.'

Sam turned the screen so they could see it.

'I know you're not feeling the movements very much,' Angelo said, 'but you can see on the screen they're definitely kicking and moving around. The heartbeats are all nice and strong.'

'You've saved my babies,' Pia said. 'I can't even begin to thank you both.'

'It's still early days,' Sam warned quietly, 'and I want you staying in the ward overnight to rest. But the signs are all looking excellent, so far.' She smiled. 'I hope you're feeling a bit less worried, now. I'm afraid I do have another patient to see, but I promise I'll call in and see you before I go home.'

'My next ward round isn't for another half an hour, so I can stay with you for a bit longer,' Angelo said. 'I'll clean up the gel, Pia, and I'll see you both back to the ward.'

Sam called in to see Pia and Tommaso after her shift, and spent a while just chatting to them; thankfully, Pia was starting to feel more foetal movements. Then she walked back to her flat and cooked herself a quick supper before calling her mum to let her know that the operation had gone well. She also emailed Will to give him a rundown of how things were going in the new department.

But, once she'd done the washing up and put everything away, she felt oddly flat.

Friday night in Florence, with nowhere to go. All the museums and tourist attractions were closed in the evenings; though, even if they had been open, Sam didn't have anybody to go with. She really didn't feel like going out and having a drink in a bar on her own. She wished she'd thought of asking some of her new colleagues if they were free that evening, before she'd left work. Yesterday evening, she'd been too busy learning Italian to think about anything else; tonight, she felt lonely.

'Enough of the pity party, Samantha Clarke,' she told herself crossly. 'It's been a long day, with a stressful operation, and you've spent most of the day practically thinking in another language. That's why you're out of sorts. What you need is a shower and an early night with a good book or a comedy.'

The shower helped, and the comedy made her laugh; though neither of them distracted her quite enough to stop her thinking about Angelo and how he'd worked seamlessly with her in Theatre. In some ways, it felt as if those two years they'd spent apart had never happened. And when they'd talked in the kitchen, there had been a moment when their eyes had met. When he'd said it was good working with her again and she'd stupidly burbled about them working well together. She'd meant professionally: of *course* she'd meant professionally. But for a second she'd seen a glint in his eye that told her he'd remembered the personal side, too. All the old feelings. The feelings for him she'd thought she'd buried had flooded back as if they'd never gone away, and she'd had to look away, not wanting him to see.

And maybe that was the real reason she felt so out of sorts. Because seeing Angelo again had brought home how much she'd loved him—and how much she'd missed him.

She spent a restless night, and was awake a good hour before her alarm. Maybe a run would sort her out; the endorphins might boost her mood. She brushed her teeth, changed into her running gear and headed out along the banks of the Arno. She'd been running for about ten minutes when she heard her name being called.

Stopping, she looked round, and saw Angelo.

Her heart skipped a beat. Even in ancient, slightly scruffy jogging bottoms and a faded T-shirt, he looked gorgeous. She'd always loved the way his hair was so easily mussed: as her best friend had once pointed out, he looked like a Raphael cherub.

'I would ask if you were out for a run, like me, but it's pretty obvious what you're doing,' he said with a smile. 'I assume your flat must be nearby?'

She nodded. 'And you obviously live near here, or you wouldn't be out for a run here.'

'Yes. The river walk is good for running, as long as you go early—that way you can avoid the crowds,' he said. 'If you head west, Cascine Park is pretty, or if you want a challenge you can cross the river and run up the Viale Michelangelo to the Piazzale, and you'll get stunning views of the city as a reward for running up a hill.'

'Thanks for the tips,' she said. 'I'll try to remember that for the future.'

'Are you due at the hospital, this morning?' he asked.

'Yes. Are you?'

He nodded, and glanced at his watch. 'Do you have plans, or would you like to join me for breakfast?'

She could make an excuse and say that she needed to finish her run. But her path would still cross with his at the hospital, and he'd realise she'd been trying to avoid him outside work, which would make it feel even more awkward.

Perhaps having breakfast with him would be a good idea. If they were in a neutral space, she could make it clear that she saw him only as a colleague. Even though, if she was honest with herself, that wasn't quite the truth. Seeing him again had made her feel so mixed-up.

She took a deep breath. Might as well face

the other bit head-on. 'Would your partner mind me joining you for breakfast?'

'There isn't anyone to mind who I have breakfast with,' he said.

Angelo was single?

That was a shock. She'd assumed that he'd started dating someone else at some point in the last two years. Then again, she knew from experience that he didn't commit, or maybe it was just that she'd been the one he hadn't wanted to commit to.

'Just to be clear, I'm asking you to breakfast as a new colleague who's just moved to the area and my boss has asked me to help you settle in,' he added.

Was that his way of telling her she didn't have to worry that he was trying to reignite their old relationship? And maybe this would give them a chance to work out how they were going to handle things.

'In that case,' she said, 'breakfast would be lovely. And I'll do the rest of my run later today.'

He took her to a café not far from the Duomo.

'This is my bill,' she said as they reached the doorway. 'And that's not negotiable. It's a condition.'

'You always were independent.' He shrugged. 'OK. Thank you. I'll have pancakes with sliced bananas, walnuts and caramel sauce, please, and a skinny cappuccino.'

She blinked. 'You haven't even looked at the menu.'

'Everyone orders pancakes, here,' he said. 'It's the house speciality. The coffee's good here, too.'

She ordered pancakes and coffee for both of them, while he found a quiet table in the corner.

'How are you settling in to Florence?' he asked when she joined him.

'Fine, thanks,' she said. 'My flat's lovely, and the hospital seems a good place to work—it's a nice team.'

'It is,' he said. 'I've been here a year, now, and I'm really enjoying it.'

The waitress brought their coffee, and Sam took a sip to bolster her courage, enjoying the slight bitterness of the brew. 'When I agreed to come here, I wasn't expecting you to be part of the team,' she said.

'When Ric told me your name, I was sure it was just a coincidence,' he said. 'Until I looked you up on the hospital website.'

So he'd had time to prepare himself for seeing her again.

Would she even have come here, if she'd known it would mean working with him for three months? Her first reaction would probably have been to refuse, but then again this might give her the chance for closure.

'So are you still with Greg?' he asked.

She stared at him, slightly taken aback. How had he known about Greg? Had he stayed in touch with some of his old friends in London and they'd told him she was dating someone else? Not that it mattered. 'No,' she said. 'He was a really lovely guy, but it just didn't work out.' Mainly because she'd dated him on the rebound, trying to get over the man who sat opposite her right now.

It hadn't worked.

'Nowadays, I'm completely focused on my career,' she said, wanting to make the point.

'Me, too.'

So they were on the same page. 'Did you get everything sorted out in Rome?' she asked.

His eyes widened. 'Rome?'

'The family stuff you went to sort out.'

'Yes,' he said, his voice suddenly clipped.

But he didn't elaborate, and it felt too intrusive to ask anything more, when he was sending out such obvious 'keep off' signals.

The silence was excruciating. Which was sad, because in their two years together, they'd never stopped talking. They'd been so in tune: which made that phone call all the harder to understand. It had come out of nowhere and Sam still didn't understand why.

Had he met someone else? She didn't think so, because Angelo wasn't the type to lie or cheat. But she really couldn't work out what had gone wrong.

Fortunately the pancakes arrived, to distract them from the awkward silence.

'You're right. They're excellent,' she said after her first taste.

'Good.' He tackled his own pancakes.

Maybe it was the carbs doing the hard work for them, but the silence between them gradually became easier. She sneaked tiny glances at him, wondering what was going on in his head. He was still the most gorgeous man she'd ever met, from the curve of his mouth to those ridiculously long eyelashes. But it wasn't just his looks; the Angelo she'd fallen in love with had been bright and passionate, and his enthusiasm for the Romans and his heritage had ignited her own interest. She'd found history a bit dull, at school, but Angelo had made it come alive for her. He'd made a list of every single bit of Roman London that could be visited: not just the pieces of Roman wall that still stood around the city and in basements, but also the amphitheatre under the Guildhall, as well as the villa with its hypocaust in Billingsgate. He'd done the same in Paris, insisting on going to Cluny to see the Roman baths as well as walking hand in hand round the art galleries with her so they could enjoy the Monets.

Maybe that was a way back to some kind of friendship. 'So you've been here a year?' she asked.

'Yes.' He looked slightly wary.

'I assume you've found every single bit of Roman remains in the city?'

The wariness dissolved. 'Most of them,' he said with a grin. 'There's a Roman temple beneath the Duomo—hence the mosaics. The main Roman forum was at the Piazza della Repubblica, there was an amphitheatre near Piazza Santa Croce, and there are the ruins of a theatre under the Palazzo Vecchio.'

'And you've got a list?'

He smiled. 'You remember my lists?'

She nodded. 'You taught me a lot I didn't know about London.'

He looked thoughtful. 'Is this your first visit to Florence?'

'Yes.' She hadn't been back to Italy since she'd gone to Venice with him.

'Maybe I can show you around when we're off duty,' he said.

Was this another example of him being a kind colleague, or was there more to it than that? Was he, too, reflecting on the fact that they were both single, and maybe wondering if they could repair the damage between them? Her skin tingled at the idea.

'Exploring a new city with someone who knows it, rather than a guidebook, means you get to find the interesting bits more quickly,' he said.

The anticipation flattened before it had a chance to rise much further. The way he was talking, it didn't sound as if he was asking her out on a date.

'And we're colleagues.'

Definitely not a date, then. Which the sensible side of her knew was a good thing, because dating him last time round had left her with a broken heart, but part of her felt disappointed.

'I know I hurt you, Sam,' he said, 'and I'm so very sorry for that, but maybe we can find our way back to some kind of friendship. It'll make things easier for both of us at the hospital.'

And maybe it would give her some closure, too. Maybe, if they became friends again, she could finally let herself move on from him instead of wondering where it all went wrong and coming up with a blank. 'All right,' she said. 'Offer accepted.'

'Are you busy after work today?' he asked.

'I was going to finish my run,' she said, not wanting to seem too eager.

'If you wouldn't mind going for a walk instead,' he said, 'there's a public garden I'd like to take you to see. It's pretty special at this time of year.'

'All right,' she said.

'Then I'll meet you outside the hospital after our shift.' He glanced at his watch. 'Thank you for breakfast, Sam. I need to shower and change before work, so I'll catch up with you at the hospital.'

'Starting with the Bianchis,' she said. 'I want to do another scan this morning and check the babies' hearts.'

'OK.' He smiled at her. 'It's good to be working with you again.'

'And you,' she said politely, even though right now she felt too confused to know whether seeing him again would be a good thing or a bad.

CHAPTER FOUR

ANGELO TURNED THE temperature down on the shower, hoping the coolness of the water would do something to restore his common sense.

It didn't help.

All he could think about was what Sam had told him: she was single.

And she'd agreed to spend time with him today, after work.

OK, so he'd suggested it in terms of a colleague showing her round the city. And he'd told her that he was focused on his career.

It was all true. Up to a point.

But he'd never forgotten the woman he'd fallen in love with. The slightly shy doctor he'd met when he'd moved from Hampstead to the London Victoria. He'd been attracted to her right from the very first moment, and not just because she was pretty; there was a warmth and sweetness about her that had drawn him.

He'd asked her to join him for a drink after work. She'd refused, and the hospital grapevine had told him that her younger brother had recently died. Knowing it was the wrong time to be pushy, he'd made friends with her instead. Over the next few months she'd gradually opened up to him; then, the night of the hospital's Valentine ball, he'd kissed her for the first time.

They'd quickly become inseparable, until the day his uncle had phoned him about his dad's addiction problem. Ironically, Sam was the one person who would've understood and given him sound advice about helping an addict; but how could he have opened up her wounds, knowing that her brother had accidentally overdosed on cocaine? He'd given her a vague story about needing to sort out some family stuff in Rome; when it was clear that his dad needed him to stay, Angelo had made the phone call to break up with Sam. He'd lost his mum, he'd lost his dad, and if Sam walked away from him it would be too much. Better to end it now than risk losing his heart completely.

Every word, every lie he'd told, had shredded his heart a little more: but wasn't it better that she should believe him shallow and callous than for her to get dragged into his family's problems and relieve the misery of her own past? When he'd told her he didn't love her, he'd almost stumbled over the words, but it was the only way to keep her away. To keep them both safe.

But now she was back.

And he was still lying to her, claiming that he saw her as just a colleague.

If they were to have any chance of getting true closure on the past and moving forwards—maybe together—then he needed to tell her the truth. But he needed to find the right words, so he didn't hurt her even more.

He towelled himself dry, dressed and headed for the hospital. Before his ward rounds, he dropped in to see the Bianchis.

'Good morning. How are you feeling, Pia?' he asked.

'Much more comfortable, thank you,' Pia said. She bit her lip. 'But the babies still aren't moving as much as I expected.'

'I know you're booked in for another foetal echocardiogram this morning before you see us,' he said, 'but for now let's have a listen.' He checked with the Pinard stethoscope—to his relief, everything sounded normal, but he knew that Pia was worried. 'It all sounds fine, but I'm going to get another scanner rather than making you try and be a contortionist,' he said, and fetched the portable Doppler scanner, knowing that Pia and Tommaso both needed the reassurance of hearing their babies' heartbeats. 'Here we go. One heartbeat, nice and steady.' He moved the head of the Doppler. 'Twin two.' He smiled. 'And, finally, baby three.'

The Bianchis both looked relieved. 'They're holding on,' Tommaso said.

'They're doing fine,' Angelo reassured them. 'So now you can try to relax during the scans this morning, and I'll see you with Sam a bit later, OK?'

When he'd finished doing the ward rounds, he caught up with Sam in her office.

'Just the man I wanted to see,' she said.

For a moment, it felt as if they were back in London. That she too had lived for the moments when they were together.

But of course it wasn't. She'd simply been expecting him to join her for the Bianchis' appointment this morning. When she added, 'I've just had the Bianchi triplets' scans through,' it confirmed why she'd wanted to see him. Obviously. And he needed to stop being ridiculous.

'I saw Pia and Tommaso first thing,' he said. 'Pia was worrying earlier that she couldn't feel the babies moving very much, so I checked their heartbeats. I used the portable Doppler so the Bianchis could hear the heartbeats for themselves.'

'Good call,' she said. 'Have a look at the echo results and see what you think.' She brought them up on screen.

Angelo studied them. 'That's wonderful,' he said. 'I can't believe how much difference there is since yesterday.'

'It's pretty dramatic,' she agreed.

'You know, doing the laser ablation felt almost as if I was waving a magic wand,' he said.

She nodded. 'That's what I love about this field of medicine. We're making such a huge difference to the parents of babies who weren't very likely to make it without our intervention. We're giving the parents hope and the babies a real chance.'

He knew she meant a general 'we' but, again, this felt personal. As if she were talking about just the two of them, and it made him feel warm from his very core. 'Yes,' he agreed.

'Ready for to see the Bianchis?' she asked.

He nodded. 'I'll call them in.'

Pia and Tommaso still looked slightly anxious when they walked into the consulting room.

'So how are you feeling, Pia?' Sam asked.

'OK. Well, scared,' Pia admitted. 'Even though we heard their hearts beating, I guess I worry that…' She stopped, clearly not wanting to voice her fears in case talking about them made the worst happen.

'Angelo and I have reviewed your echo results, and we're really pleased,' Sam said gently. 'Let's do the ultrasound so we can see what's happening.'

Angelo assisted, squeezing Pia's hand and Tommaso's shoulder in reassurance as Sam stroked the transceiver over Pia's abdomen. He was pretty sure this would all be fine, but there was always that tiny, tiny margin of doubt.

But then Sam angled the screen towards the Bianchis. 'Twin one. Twin two. And baby three.'

Pia burst into tears—happy tears and Tommaso hugged her. Angelo couldn't help wrapping his own arms round Sam, overcome with relief and joy that the procedure had worked so well, and for a moment Sam hugged him back.

Something shifted in the region of his heart, and he pulled back. Her gorgeous grey eyes were wide with an emotion he couldn't quite name. Had she, too, felt more than the joy of the moment? Her lips parted, and for a crazy moment the whole world disappeared and it was just the two of them in the room.

But then Pia asked, 'So it's all as it should be?'

Sam shifted back into professional mode. 'Yes. They've all got good movements, and more importantly the scans earlier showed me the blood flow and I'm very happy with it. So your job now is to relax, rest, and do something that will help distract you from worrying.'

'And we'll see you for a regular check-up on Friday,' Angelo said, battening down his feelings and going into professional mode, too. 'Obviously, if you have any concerns before then, call us.'

'I'm pleased to say we're happy to send you home,' Sam said with a smile, 'provided you rest.'

'I'll make sure she rests,' Tommaso said.

After clinic, Sam was called in to help with an emergency delivery of a baby in distress, and Angelo didn't see her again before the end of his shift.

He waited for her outside the hospital, as they'd arranged.

She'd agreed to go out with him this evening—strictly as friends—but she'd had a day to think about it, between seeing patients. Would she have changed her mind? He knew she'd turn up; she'd always been meticulous about keeping her word and he didn't think that would've changed. But she might have had second thoughts about spending the evening with him. Especially after that hug. He could probably explain it away as relief, but they'd both know it wasn't.

Would it make Sam back away?

Adrenalin shimmered through him, making him feel as nervous as if this was a first date. Which was ridiculous. This was merely a situation where one colleague was showing another around a new city, that was all, he told himself.

And then he rolled his eyes. Who was he trying to kid? He hadn't been able to stop thinking about Sam since he'd seen her again on Thursday morning. Though, until he'd been honest with her about why he'd walked away from her in the first place, he couldn't really ask for her forgiveness. And that was a conversation where he didn't have a clue how to start.

Angelo looked in a world of his own, leaning against the wall near the hospital entrance and gazing into the distance. Was he regretting his offer to take her to show her the gardens and wishing he hadn't burdened himself with her company? Sam wondered. Or was he, too, thinking about their situation and wondering quite where they went from here? Was he, too, thinking about the moment they'd hugged each other and the way their closeness had triggered all the memories of their past?

She walked up to him. 'Penny for them?'

He jumped slightly, then looked at her and smiled. 'I'd be overcharging you,' he said. 'Sorry. Miles away. Are you still OK to go and see the gardens?'

His expression was completely inscrutable, and she had no idea whether this was his way of giving them both a let-out, or whether he was simply trying not to put any pressure on her.

Maybe he, too, needed closure. Maybe this would give them the opportunity they needed to really talk, and finally put the past behind them. 'I'm fine to go, if you are,' she said.

He smiled, then. She'd forgotten how his smile could make her feel as if the world was all lit up.

'Let's head into town,' he said.

He pointed out some of the buildings to her as they headed into the historic centre. 'We're going to take the quicker route up to the Piazzale Michelangelo today,' he said, 'but I can show you where the running route comes out.'

'Thanks. That'd be good.'

Once they'd crossed over the Ponte Vecchio, they walked alongside the river for a while.

'The Bardini Gardens are also worth a look, when you've got a free afternoon,' he said, pointing out the entrance to the gardens as they passed. 'They've got a tunnel of those purple flowers you like. The ones you once dragged me to see in Notting Hill.'

'Wisteria,' she said with a smile. 'And you have to admit it was gorgeous.' She still had pictures somewhere of them together next to the wisteria, with the white-painted walls of the house a perfect backdrop to the flowers. 'So where are we going?'

'The Giardino dell'Iris—the Iris Gardens,' he said. 'The gardens are only open while the irises are blooming, so you're in Florence at the perfect time.'

They walked up to a honey-coloured stone archway. 'This is Porta San Miniato, one of the gates in the old city wall,' he said. 'And we're going to walk up the steps along the outside of the rose garden.'

The steps looked wide and shallow, but she soon discovered that the hill was steeper than it looked—and a lot longer.

'Don't turn round to look until you get to the top,' he said. 'I promise the view's worth it.'

Sam had always enjoyed walking through a city with Angelo. Whenever they'd taken a mini break together, he'd researched the city thoroughly beforehand and made a list of places he wanted to visit, so they could make the most of their time and see as much as possible.

He'd done the same in London, making a list of the places he wanted to visit, and splitting them between rainy and sunny days. At the London Victoria, they'd sorted out the rosters so they were off duty at the same time, and they'd gradually worked their way through Angelo's list, seeing everything from the weird jars of specimens at the Hunterian Museum and the butterflies at the Horniman, through to the bluebells in Highgate Wood and the summer roses in Regent's Park.

She'd just bet he had an amazing list for Florence.

Maybe he'd share the list with her, if she asked—even if he didn't want to go to the different places with her.

At the top of the steps, he gestured to the bronze replica of Michelangelo's David. 'Keep walking over to the statue—don't look anywhere else—and *then* you can turn round.'

She did, and gave a sharp intake of breath as she saw the view of the city, with the mountains behind it as a backdrop. 'That's so pretty, with all the old buildings running along the side of the river. I know that's the Duomo and the bell tower—but what's the other tall tower?'

'The Palazzo Vecchio, which is definitely worth a visit,' he said. 'There are some great sculptures, and there's a good view from the top of the tower.'

'I'll add it to my list of things to see,' she said.

From his expression, she guessed that he, too, was remembering his old London list and how they'd worked their way through it. Would he offer to join her with her list in Florence, or would he keep his distance?

'Good idea,' he said, and she felt the lurch of disappointment in her stomach. He'd clearly chosen distance.

'Let's go and look at the irises,' she said. 'I assume from the name that it's mainly irises in the garden?'

'And olive trees,' he said. 'But it's dedicated to irises, so it's only open when the flowers are blooming.'

'So why specialise in just one flower with a short blooming season? Why not plant the kind of garden that has something different every month?'

'It started out as a competition garden. Apparently there's been a competition every year for decades to produce an iris the exact shade of the red one on the Florentine coat of arms,' he explained. 'There are a couple of thousand varieties of iris, but it seems it's really hard to breed a red one.'

She frowned. 'I thought it was a lily on the Florentine coat of arms. A fleur-de-lys.'

'They look similar, but the symbol is actually inspired by an iris,' he said.

She believed him. Angelo always had done his research. Besides, the garden was pretty and she enjoyed walking round the narrow, winding stone pathways with him, shaded by olive trees. There were birds singing and flowers everywhere; as well as the shades of blue, purple, white and yellow she was used to, there were irises in shades of apricot, peach and pink, and even black. They ranged in size from the tiny ones she'd grown on a windowsill to truly gigantic, and everywhere she looked she could see frilly petals, with the grey-green leaves of the olive trees as the perfect background to the riot of colour. Behind the trees, the hills loomed, and above them fluffy white clouds scudded along a blue, blue sky.

It was idyllic. If she and Angelo had come here together when they were still a couple, she would've loved every second; it was so romantic. By the pond in the lower garden, she almost forgot herself and reached for his hand. At the last moment, she realised what she was about to do and touched his arm instead. 'Look. Dragonflies.' She indicated the blue and orange dragonflies hovering over the water.

'And the frogs are definitely trying to compete with the birds,' he said with a grin. 'I don't think I've ever heard such loud croaking.'

'Thank you for bringing me here. This is lovely.'

'I hoped you'd like it.' He smiled at her. 'There are great views from the rose garden we walked beside, too. And the Piazzale itself is a good place to sit and watch the sunset.' He wrinkled his nose. 'I should've thought to pick up some things at lunchtime for a picnic.'

A picnic at sunset. It was the sort of thing she'd once loved doing with him, but she wasn't sure she could handle it now. There would be too many memories. Too much sadness about what they'd lost. 'Maybe some other time,' she said.

'I was wondering,' he said. 'Given that you bought me breakfast, would you like to join me for dinner tonight?'

'Dinner?'

'Nothing fancy,' he said. 'I thought we could walk back down the hill. There are some good places to eat on this side of the river. And the Ponte Vecchio looks at its best around sunset.'

This wasn't a date, she reminded herself. She needed to think of him purely as a colleague she'd once known, who felt he owed her dinner in return for the breakfast she'd bought him. Besides, if she said no it meant she'd be spending another evening alone in Florence, because she hadn't arranged anything with anyone else. 'OK. That'd be nice,' she said.

Tell her now. Now, when the world was full of flowers and butterflies and sunshine. When there was enough space round them that it wouldn't become painfully intense...

But Angelo couldn't find the words. Knowing that he was being a coward and avoiding the conversation they really needed to have, he talked about the city instead. Was it his guilty conscience, or did Sam's expression say that she knew why he was keeping her at arm's length? Then again, she wasn't raising the subject, either. Maybe they'd needed time to get used to each other again before they could talk about their unfinished business.

When they'd finished looking at the irises,

they walked through the rose garden, and Sam enjoyed hearing the hum of bees and watching butterflies flit between the flowers. The scent was incredible, as were the views, and Sam took snaps to send later to her mum and Nina. Then they took a winding path back down the hill, ending up at another of the old medieval gates. Angelo led her through a maze of narrow cobbled streets, with tall buildings either side painted in tones of ochre and saffron and cream, their narrow windows flanked by shutters.

He took her to a tiny restaurant whose tables had red checked tablecloths, and there were candles stuck in raffia-covered bottles.

'The decor's a bit retro,' he said, 'but the food's fantastic.'

The waiter brought them breadsticks and explained that the day's menu was on the chalkboard; when he asked what they'd like to drink, Angelo looked at Sam. 'Chianti OK with you?' he asked.

'Lovely,' she said. 'And maybe a jug of water?'

'What do you recommend to eat tonight?' Angelo asked.

'The meatballs are good,' the waiter said. 'And for sides, the potatoes and spinach.'

'Sounds good to me,' Sam said, and Angelo ordered for both of them.

When the waiter had brought the wine, Angelo lifted his glass in a toast. '*Saluti*. Welcome to Florence, Sam.'

'*Saluti,*' she said, clinking her glass against his. 'Mmm, this is good.' She paused. 'So, as you've been here a year, I assume you've already worked your way through the places you want to see in the city?'

He grinned. 'Most of the things on my list, yes.'

'What do you recommend?'

'All the churches,' he said. 'Every one has something different, whether it's amazing sculpture or ancient frescos that look as if they were painted yesterday instead of hundreds of years ago. And it's definitely worth going up inside the Duomo, because it's fascinating to see how it was all put together, though you'll need to book a few days in advance.'

'I'll book a ticket for next week, on my day off,' she said.

'And there are Roman mosaics in the basement. Keep an eye out for the peacock.'

Sam grinned. 'Of course. Roman stuff.'

'But Florence,' he said, 'is more about the Renaissance. The Medici.'

'And the art,' she said.

'It's definitely worth buying timed tickets for the galleries,' he said. 'My favourite's the Uffizi, for the Botticellis. And, believe me, even though you might think you know what *The Birth of Venus* is like from all the reproductions, it's really something else in real life. All the little details. It's stunning.'

'I'll add that to my list.' She wondered if he was going to suggest going with her, and her stomach swooped in disappointment when he didn't. Which was crazy. They weren't even considering getting back together. He'd dumped her two years ago without any real explanation. Why would he change his mind now? And she wasn't sure she was ready to handle a conversation about what had happened. Not yet. So she deliberately kept the conversation light during dinner; the chicken and ricotta meatballs in tomato sauce were excellent, along with the side dishes of tiny roasted potatoes with rosemary and garlicky, buttery spinach.

She didn't have room for pudding, but the coffee was fantastic.

They left the restaurant just in time to see the sun setting across the river. The amazing colours in the sky were reflected on the river, and the Ponte Vecchio had turned golden in the sunlight. 'I need to take a snap of this for

Mum and Nina,' she said. 'I can see why so many people take photographs of the bridge. It's so pretty.'

'The ground floor is shops and the middle floor is housing, but the top level's the Vasari Corridor,' he said. 'It was built for one of the Medici dukes to connect the Palazzo Pitti with the Palazzo Vecchio. They made all the owners of the towers on the bridge agree to let them build the corridor through their property—except for the Mannelli family, who refused, so the corridor had to go round their tower.'

'Someone actually stood up to the Medici and survived?' She raised her eyebrows.

'Surprisingly, yes,' he said.

When they sun had finally set, he turned to her. 'I know you can look after yourself and Florence is a safe city, but I'd still rather walk you home.'

'I won't argue,' she said, 'because you're saving me having to get my phone out to check that I'm remembering the right way to get home.'

At the door to her building, she said, 'Thank you for this evening. It's been really nice.'

'I enjoyed it, too,' he said.

Should she ask him in for coffee?

If they'd been new colleagues, new friends,

she probably would have asked him in. But this was Angelo. They had history. And they couldn't turn back the clock—even though it would be oh, so easy to lean towards him and kiss him on the cheek, to let one thing lead to another...

And then things would get really complicated.

Better to let things be. She was only here for eleven more weeks, and they were colleagues. She couldn't afford to let her feelings get in the way.

'I'll see you at work on Monday,' she said.

'Enjoy your day off,' he said politely. 'See you Monday.'

Angelo waited until Sam had closed the door behind her before he headed back to his own flat. Spending the evening with her had been bittersweet; the teasing light in her eyes when she'd asked him about the Roman bits of Florence had brought back so many memories of trips he'd taken with her to see Roman ruins. London, Paris, Bath, the Roman villa at Fishbourne...

And he'd been so close to kissing her goodnight on her doorstep. If he'd just leaned forward—would she have met his lips? Would she have kissed him back? Would she have asked him in, to spend more time together?

But there was a huge, huge boulder in their path: the way he'd dumped her, two years ago. He really needed to apologise properly and tell her why he'd really left London. He knew he should've done it this evening; except he'd been enjoying spending time with her and he hadn't wanted to spoil it by bringing up past hurts.

'You're such a coward, Angelo Brunelli,' he told himself. 'You can't turn back time. But you can't go forward until you've sorted it out.'

He just had to find the right words. Somehow.

Sunday was another gorgeously sunny day, and Sam spent the day exploring Florence. She'd bought a timed ticket for the Uffizi, on Angelo's recommendation, and enjoyed the gallery hugely. The exhibits were stunning and, as he'd told her the previous day, the Botticelli paintings were amazing in real life, full of tiny details. The gallery itself was a work of art, too, with its painted ceilings and marble floors, and Sam loved the dome with its ceiling covered in shells. She lingered by the windows, enjoying the views over the city, then sat on the café's balcony in the sunshine, next to the terracotta pots filled with herbs and shrubs, sipping coffee while she looked across the rooftops to the Duomo and the bell tower.

Yet, although she was enjoying herself, she was aware there was something missing.

Angelo.

Which was ridiculous. They hadn't been together for two years. She'd moved on and, was focussing on her career.

Though last night had reminded her of so many days out she'd spent with Angelo, discovering nerdy things together and delighting in obscure facts. If he'd been with her today, she knew he would've told her something about every single room or exhibit in the Uffizi.

But, if he'd wanted to spend time with her, surely he would've said so? The fact that he hadn't made it clear he didn't want to resurrect the past.

They'd established a good working relationship, now they'd moved beyond the initial awkwardness.

Wanting more than that—well, she would just be setting herself up for disappointment.

She was going to enjoy her temporary secondment, make friends with her new colleagues and explore her temporary home.

And then she'd go back to London and forget about Angelo Brunelli.

CHAPTER FIVE

FOR THE NEXT WEEK, Sam was busy at the hospital; when she wasn't seeing new cases in the foetal medicine unit, she worked with some of the more complex cases in the main maternity department. Over the next few days, she got to know her new colleagues a lot better and even spent a couple of evenings out with some of them, enjoying drinks and a meal and learning more about Florence. She noticed that Angelo didn't join them; was he trying to avoid her outside work? So much for thinking that they'd be able to get some kind of closure and find their way to a friendship. Perhaps he hadn't meant it after all?

Ten more weeks.

She could keep a professional attitude towards him for ten more weeks.

On the Friday morning, the Bianchis came in for a check-up and scan, so Sam had to work with Angelo.

'I'm really pleased with the way things are going,' she said when she'd finished doing the scan. 'One of the twins is still smaller, but he's starting to catch up.'

'I still worry,' Pia admitted.

'Of course you do. That's completely normal,' Angelo reassured her with a smile.

'Will you be here when the babies arrive?' Pia asked Sam.

'You're twenty-three weeks pregnant, and I'm here for another ten weeks,' Sam said. 'Given our plan to get you to thirty-three weeks if we can, I'm pretty sure I'll be here. And if I'm not on duty when you deliver, I'll come in anyway. I'll make sure there's a note on the file to call me.' She smiled. 'Apart from anything else, I can never resist a cuddle with a newborn. And in your case that's three cuddles, so that's a real bonus.'

Pia looked pleased. 'It wouldn't be the same without you there.'

'That's kind.' Sam smiled. 'Is there anything either of you want to ask me?'

Pia and Tommaso looked at each other, and then shook their heads. 'I think you covered everything.'

'Then we'll see you next week,' Sam said. 'Take things easy.'

'I'll make sure she does,' Tommaso promised.

* * *

Angelo was busy catching up with paperwork in the early afternoon when Lidia put her head round the door. 'I need you to do a scan, and possibly a section.'

'What's up?'

'Raffaella Costa's just come into the labour ward. She's thirty-nine weeks, but the baby's breech.'

Angelo thought back. 'Am I right in remembering that her baby seemed to have a plexus cyst earlier on, but it sorted itself out?'

Lidia nodded. 'But the baby's head feels a bit large. I'm not happy.'

If there was fluid on the baby's brain, it could cause the baby to have breathing problems after birth. 'Can you get the portable scanner?' he asked. 'I'll check the notes, then grab Sam and brief her.'

She was in clinic, and he felt guilty about interrupting, but at the same time he knew that this was going to be a complex case—one where he really needed her expertise.

'I'm so sorry to interrupt,' he said to the parents in her consulting room, 'but I need a very quick word with Dr Clarke.'

'Problem?' Sam asked when they were in the corridor.

'Potentially, yes. Lidia has a mum who's just come in—Raffaella Costa. She's thirty-nine weeks pregnant. At twenty weeks, the scan showed the baby had a plexus cyst on her head, but it resolved naturally and her last scan, at thirty weeks, was fine.' He grimaced. 'But Lidia's not happy. She feels the baby's head is too large.'

'Potentially fluid on the brain?' Sam asked.

He nodded, knowing that Sam would be aware of what complications might follow on from that. 'And the baby's breech. I'm going to do a scan, but I think it's quite likely that Rafaella will need an emergency section. Given your experience with more complex births, we could do with your input.'

'OK. I assume the neonatal team are on standby?' Sam asked.

'Already sorted.'

'Right. I'll finish up with my parents here. Then I'll prime Carla on reception that I might need to either get the parents to wait a bit for the rest of my afternoon's clinic, reschedule their appointments or maybe see someone else if Carla can get cover. Once that's sorted, I'll come in to check the scan results with you. Which room will you be in?'

'Room four,' he said.

'OK. Give me a few minutes.'

Angelo had just done the scan, confirming that there was indeed fluid on the baby's brain, and was telling the Costas that he wanted to do a Caesarean section when Sam came in. He introduced her quickly to Raffaella and her husband Mauro. 'This is Dr Samantha Clarke, a specialist from England who's with us for the next three months,' he said. 'Sam, this is Raffaella and Mauro Costa.'

'Hello,' Sam said with a smile. 'I'm here to support you along with Angelo and Lidia. Angelo's told me the history of your pregnancy, and I'm sorry you've had so much worry.'

'I so wanted a normal birth,' Raffaella said. 'But Lidia and Angelo say I need a section because the baby's breech.'

'Babies never do anything according to plan,' Sam said. 'I don't think I've met anyone whose birth went as they'd planned it, and plenty of my mums have made their birth plan into a paper plane, over the years. From what I've just seen on the scan, I agree with Lidia and Angelo that a section would be safest for you and for the baby.'

Raffaella bit her lip. 'Is she going to make it? When she had that cyst, the information leaflet said she might have fluid on her brain, and that might mean she can't breathe when she's born. And if she can't breathe… If she…' Her voice choked off.

'That's why we'll have the neonatal team in with us, to make sure your baby has the right support. Plenty of babies need a little bit of help after the birth,' Sam reassured her. 'Don't try to think of what *might* happen— that's way too scary. Focus on the fact that Lidia's a great midwife; she's kept a careful eye on you and she isn't going to let you take unnecessary risks.'

'But I can have a Caesarean section and still be awake, can't I?' Raffaella asked.

'Given that this is an emergency section, we'd rather do it under a general anaesthetic,' Angelo said. 'It's safer for both you and the baby.'

Raffaella's eyes widened. 'Will Mauro still be there for the birth?'

'No, but he'll be able to see the baby very soon afterwards,' Sam reassured her.

Raffaella clutched Mauro's hand. 'Promise me you'll take a picture of her, Mauro. In case—' her voice cracked '—in case our little girl doesn't make it before I wake up.'

'She'll make it,' Mauro said. But his tone was hollow.

'Promise me,' Raffaella insisted.

'I promise,' he said, his face looking haunted.

'Try not to worry,' Sam said. 'You'll be cuddling your daughter very soon. I'm just going to sort out my appointments for the afternoon while you see the anaesthetist, and I'll be there in Theatre, OK?'

Though Angelo recognised that tiny pleat between Sam's eyes. Something was definitely worrying her. But, despite the complication of a breech birth and the size of the baby's head, the Caesarean section itself should be relatively straightforward.

'What's wrong?' he asked when she was back from sorting out her appointments and they were scrubbing in.

'I…' She shook her head. 'It's fine.'

Her smile was a bit too brittle for his liking, but now wasn't the time to push her to talk. They had a baby to deliver safely.

The anaesthetist had already done her work and Raffaella was on the operating table. Sam did the 'knife check'—making sure the consent form had been signed, confirming Raffaella's identity and running through the risk of a bleed; then Raffaella was prepped and draped for the operation. Sam checked with the anaesthetist that they were ready to go; when the anaesthetist nodded, Sam made the incision and between them she and Angelo performed the Caesarean section.

When Sam lifted the baby out, the baby's head was definitely bigger than average; she was covered in vernix, and, more worryingly, she was silent. Angelo couldn't see any sign of her breathing. Her skin was blue, and he wasn't happy with the look of her muscle tone. It was normal for a baby born after a Caesarean section to have a slightly lower Apgar score—the first assessment of the baby's health scored on the appearance, pulse, grimace response, activity and respiration—but this baby needed resuscitating.

Sam removed the placenta, leaving the cord attached to the baby without clamping it; Angelo knew in a minute or so it would be time to clamp and cut the cord, making sure the baby had the optimum blood from the placenta.

Lidia took the baby from them and began rubbing her vigorously with a towel. 'One-minute Apgar score of three,' she said.

Breathe, baby, Angelo thought. *Please breathe. Breathe and pink up. Cry. Move your arms. Grimace.*

Sam's face had lost all colour, beneath her surgical mask; he was pretty sure she was as worried about the baby as he was. She did the routine check of Raffaella's reproductive organs, then started to sew up the incision she'd made in the uterus. Angelo admired her quick, deft, work, but he was aware that both of them were waiting anxiously to hear the baby's first cry.

The longer it took, the more help the baby was likely to need.

He remembered the desperation in Raffaella's eyes when she'd asked Mauro to take a photo of the baby. Her conviction that their daughter wouldn't make it. Had it been maternal instinct?

Please, baby, just breathe, he begged silently.

'Cord, please, Angelo,' Lidia said.

He clamped the cord and cut it. One of the neonatal team had put an oxygen mask over the baby's face.

Still there was no sound other than the low, worried murmuring of Lidia and the neonatal team. There was no sign of the first, stuttering cry that they were all desperate to hear.

Sam met his gaze for a moment, and her eyes were suspiciously shiny; then she blinked and continued stitching.

Please let the baby make it. Please.

Angelo continued to worked alongside Sam,

handing her the things he knew she'd need the moment before she needed to ask him for them.

And then finally, just as he thought the neo-natal team would have to intubate the baby to support her breathing, there was a faint cry.

'Good girl,' Lidia crooned. 'That's what we all wanted to hear. Five-minute Apgar score of five.'

Sam said nothing, but she stopped stitching and closed her eyes for a moment in apparent relief. Five out of ten still wasn't as high as they would've liked, but it was a move in the right direction, and Angelo knew Lidia and the neonatal team would do another score in three minutes' time to keep a check on the baby's condition.

'We're going to take her to Neonatal Intensive Care to warm up a bit and help her breathe,' the neonatal specialist said. 'And then we'll sort out a head scan. I'm not happy with the size of the baby's head, either—I think you might be right about fluid on the brain.'

'OK. I'll get a message to her dad—he's in the waiting room,' Angelo said. 'Can he come and see her?'

'Of course,' the neonatal specialist said.

'Well done, everyone,' Sam said, her voice

heartfelt. She looked at Angelo. 'I'm OK to finish here. Go and see Mauro and tell him the good news—that he has a little girl.'

Mauro was pacing up and down the waiting room.

'Is—?' He stopped, clearly terrified of the answer. Had the baby made it?

'Your daughter's on her way to the neonatal unit to warm up a bit and to have a little bit of help breathing,' Angelo reassured him. 'Right now, she's holding her own.'

Mauro sagged in relief. 'I was trying to be strong for Raffaella's sake, but deep down I thought the same as her, that the baby wouldn't make it.' A tear slid down his cheek. 'Is my wife all right?'

'Sam's finishing sewing her up, and then we're going to wake her up and take her through to the recovery room. You can go and see the baby now, if you like. Take that photograph for Raffaella; by the time you come back, she'll be awake and desperate to see the baby.'

'Thank you,' Mauro said hoarsely. 'If the baby hadn't made it, I don't know what…'

'I know,' Angelo said, patting his arm. 'The team's going to organise a scan of the baby's head, later today. But whatever happens we're here to support you, OK?'

When he got back to Theatre, Raffaella was in the recovery room, coming round from the anaesthetic. He went to find Sam, to debrief her; she was scrubbing out, and he noticed that her eyes were wet.

'What's wrong?' he asked.

'Nothing. I'm fine.'

He knew she wasn't telling the truth. 'Sam,' he said gently, 'you looked worried sick in Theatre and you're crying now.'

'Relief,' she said. 'Because for a while there I didn't think the baby was going to make it.'

He'd felt that same fear, but he wasn't in tears. There was more to this than met the eye. 'What happened?' he asked softly.

'If you must know, I had a case, a couple of years back,' she said, 'where the baby was a breech birth with an emergency section. The baby didn't make it. And this time we had the extra complication, with the extra fluid on the baby's head. I don't often lose a baby, so doing the section brought back some tough memories.'

Acting entirely on impulse, Angelo slid his arms round her and held her close for a moment.

Sam relaxed against him, and he couldn't stop himself resting his cheek against her hair, stroking her back.

To have her in his arms again, after all these years… It felt like paradise.

Did it feel like that for her, too? Had she missed him as much as he'd missed her?

Then Sam's muscles tensed, and it brought Angelo sharply back to the present. This was incredibly inappropriate. Unprofessional. No matter how upset she was, he shouldn't be hugging her in the scrub room. He released her and took a step back. 'Sorry. I just thought you could do with a hug from a colleague,' he said, feeling the blood rush to his face.

'Thank you,' she mumbled, not looking at him.

'I, um…' Since when had he been this incoherent? 'I'd better let you get back to your clinic.'

'Uh-huh,' she said.

Keep it professional. Focus on the patients, he reminded himself. 'Mauro's with the baby. He's going to come back to the recovery room when he's taken a picture for Raffaella.'

'That's good,' she said. 'Catch you later.'

That hug had really thrown Sam. A moment of comfort when she'd needed it—just as Angelo had comforted her on rough days years ago, days when she'd missed Dominic and struggled to come to terms with his overdose. Angelo had made her see that her best *had* been good enough, that nobody else could've done more to stop Dominic on his tragic path.

That brief physical contact in the scrub room had brought back so many memories, so many times when Angelo had held her. And she missed it. Missed it so much, it was a physical ache.

Right now, they were trying to work their way back to some sort of friendship. But could it be more than that? Could they find their way back to the closeness they'd once had? Or would she be setting herself up for more heartache? She was only here temporarily and her career—her life—was back in London.

It was hard to think straight. She needed to focus and get on with her job. Work, at least, was safe.

She apologised to the parents who'd had to wait while she'd been in Theatre, and stayed well after the end of her shift to make sure she caught up with everyone. Then she headed through to the neonatal intensive care unit to see how the Costas were doing.

Raffaella and Mauro were sitting either side of a tiny cot, each with a finger held by the baby.

'Sorry I couldn't get here earlier,' she said. 'I was in clinic.'

'Don't apologise. We know you put all your other mums on hold so you could deliver Paola,' Raffaella said. 'And I'm so, so grateful. Lidia told me, she wasn't doing so well at first.' A tear trickled down her cheek. 'If we'd lost her…'

'I know,' Sam said gently. 'You said her name's Paola?'

'After my grandmother,' Mauro said.

'That's lovely.' Sam smiled. 'So how's she doing? How was the scan?'

Raffaella swallowed hard. 'They said there are cavities in the brain, and the fluid acts as a shock absorber, but Paola's got a lot more fluid there than she should have.'

'That sometimes happens when a baby's had a plexus cyst,' Sam said.

'They said she's at risk of having seizures and learning difficulties,' Mauro said, his voice cracking slightly. 'Our little girl.'

'That's an awful lot to take in,' Sam said. 'I'm sure the team here has already told you that "learning difficulties" is a very broad spectrum. Try not to think the worst. It might simply be that Paola doesn't crawl or sit up as early as other babies do, or she might be a bit slower to start talking.' Or it could be a lot more serious; right now it was too early to tell. 'But it's early days and there's a lot of support you can access.'

'We're just grateful she's here,' Raffaella said. 'I was so scared we were going to lose her.'

Sam peered into the cot. 'She's beautiful. I can see both of you in her.'

'Thank you for all you did,' Mauro said.

'I'm so sorry you couldn't be awake for the birth, and that Mauro couldn't cut the cord,' Sam said. 'I know that's really disappointing for both of you.'

'But Paola's here now. She's safe, and so's Raffaella. That's the main thing,' Mauro said.

'I'll leave you to get to know your little one,' Sam said. 'But I'll pop in to see you when I'm next in the hospital.'

When she went into the staff room, she was surprised to see Angelo there. 'I thought your shift finished ages ago.'

'It did. I was waiting for you,' he said.

She frowned. 'Why?'

'Because you've had a tough day, and in your shoes I know I could do with some company and some carbs,' he said gently. 'Do you have anything planned for this evening?'

She could fib and say that she was meeting up with some of the maternity team, but the lie would be too easily unravelled. 'No,' she admitted.

'Then how about I cook you dinner?' he asked. 'Nothing super-fancy and no strings: it'll be whatever I've got in the fridge and the freezer. Just dinner with…' He paused. 'With an old friend.'

He'd been a lot more than just an old friend, and they both knew it, but she let it slide. Even though there had been a happy ending today, the case had brought back memories of the baby who hadn't made it. It had been the first complicated operation she'd done after Dominic's death, and she'd always wondered if there was something she'd done wrong: if she'd let herself get distracted by her personal life and missed something crucial that could've made a difference. She'd been over it again and again, and eventually her boss had sat her down and told her that it wasn't her fault; whoever had performed the operation, that particular baby still wouldn't have made it because the odds had been just too high.

But Sam had never quite stopped feeling bad about it. Right now, she didn't want to be on her own and she needed something or someone to distract her.

'OK,' she said. 'Dinner would be nice. Thank you.'

Angelo waited for Sam to get her things from her locker; then they walked back to the city together.

'I'd like to contribute something to the meal,' she said.

Angelo shook his head. 'It's really nothing fancy: just gnocchi with tomato and mascarpone sauce. I made the gnocchi last week and it's in the freezer. It'll take all of five minutes from start to finish, and it's as quick to cook for two as for one.'

'Can I at least buy the wine?' she asked.

'I think I can just about afford to give you some wine,' he said drily. 'No. You're fine.'

His flat was in a quiet street, on the fourth floor of a cream-coloured building with olive-green shutters. 'I'll give you the thirty-second tour,' he said with a smile as he opened his front door. 'Bathroom.' He indicated the first door, then led her past a second door—which she assumed was his bedroom—through to the living room. 'Living room.' It had wooden parquet flooring, a comfortable sofa, a bookshelf and a coffee table; there were photographs on the mantelpiece—one of his parents that she remembered him having in London—and a couple of prints of Rome on the walls. At one end of the room there was a small table and chairs; in the middle of the room there were large glass doors. 'That's the balcony. It's just about wide enough for a table and two chairs. I thought we could eat there tonight.' He gestured through the glass doors. 'And the kitchen.' It was a narrow galley kitchen with terracotta flooring and a view of a church and the hills outside the city. She noted the fresh herbs on the windowsill. The entire flat was immaculately tidy, but it definitely felt like a home rather than a show flat.

'I'll start cooking dinner,' he said. He set water to boil in the kettle, took two portions of gnocchi from the freezer, and put two saucepans on the hob.

'Can I do anything to help?' she asked.

'You can slice some bread and take it through to the balcony,' he said. 'And maybe lay the table. The key to the door is in the dish on the table, and everything in the kitchen is in an obvious place.'

The crockery was on open shelving, the bread bin was on top of the microwave—and the top was clearly the cutting board—and she found the cutlery and a bread knife in the drawer next to the sink.

She sliced the bread and put it on a plate, then took it and the cutlery out to the balcony. The balcony ran the whole length of the living room; it had a terracotta tiled floor and wrought-iron railing. There were pots of geraniums clustered by the railing, and a bistro table with two chairs was set in the middle. The view was beautiful: the narrow street and a garden opposite that was stuffed to bursting with flowering shrubs.

When she went back to the kitchen, the gnocchi was cooking in boiling water and the tomato sauce was bubbling; Angelo was scooping out the gnocchi as they floated to the surface of the water.

'Anything else?' she asked.

'Wine. Red's in the rack, and there's a bottle of white in the fridge, so pick whichever you'd prefer and open it,' he said.

Sam had missed this kind of domesticity. Greg hadn't been interested in cooking, leaving it to her and sorting out the clearing up instead. But she'd always enjoyed working with Angelo in the kitchen; they'd been a team.

She found glasses and uncorked a bottle of red; by the time she'd done that, Angelo had added the mascarpone to the tomato sauce, added the gnocchi and filled two bowls.

'Let's go and eat,' he said, and ushered her out to the balcony.

'You've got a fabulous view,' she said.

He smiled. 'I think that goes for just about anywhere in Florence, particularly if you're on a higher floor. You get the iconic view of the rooftops, the hills and the sky—and maybe a tower or two.'

'It's a beautiful city,' she said.

'Agreed.'

'This is very good,' she said after her first taste of the gnocchi. 'You always were an excellent cook.' And the carbs were just what she needed.

He inclined his head. 'Thank you.'

To Sam's relief, Angelo kept the conversation light during dinner. She didn't have room for pudding or cheese, but she accepted the offer of coffee.

He took a deep breath, as if nerving himself to say something, and then he looked her in the eye. 'Sam. There's something I need to tell you.' He paused. 'When I left London… I lied to you.'

CHAPTER SIX

SAM STARED AT ANGELO, not quite making sense of his words. He'd lied to her? About what? And why? 'I don't understand.' She found it hard to believe that Angelo would've cheated on her; she'd been absolutely sure he was the faithful type. But what other explanation could there be? 'Are you telling me you left me for someone else—someone in Rome?'

'No. Of course there wasn't anyone else.' He frowned. 'I mean I lied about not loving you any more.'

That still didn't shed any light on it for her. Why would he lie about that? 'Why?'

'Because I was trying to do the right thing.'

She shook her head, trying to clear it. 'Right thing? For whom?' She still didn't get it. How had breaking her heart been 'the right thing' to do?

He sighed. 'I don't know how to tell you. I didn't want to hurt you.'

'But you *did* hurt me.'

'And I'm sorry. But I didn't know what to do, Sam. Whatever I did, I knew it was going to cause you pain. If I'd told you the truth, it would've...' He shook his head. 'I went for the option with the least collateral damage. I thought if I pushed you away, made you think I didn't love you any more, it would protect you.'

'Angelo, you're not making any sense at all.'

His face was filled with anguish. 'OK. I need to tell you what really happened. And I'm sorry, Sam. I'm sorry I hurt you, and I'm sorry because I know I'm about to hurt you all over again.'

Worry made her sharp. 'Just tell me.'

'The ripping-off-the-plaster quickly version? All right.' He took a deep breath. 'My dad was an addict.'

An addict.

Like her little brother had been.

And Sam could still remember the day she'd had to identify him in the mortuary. Dominic, who'd struggled so hard to stop taking the stuff, but the cocaine had finally beaten him. The boy she could remember as a newborn, when she'd taken him a teddy to welcome him to the world. All that life, all that hope, had turned into a cold body on a cold slab.

'He was taking coke?' she whispered.

'No. Codeine.'

She knew the opiate painkiller that could start to become addictive if it was used for more than a week, which was why doctors were super-careful about prescribing it. 'What happened?'

'Dad was in a car accident,' he said. 'It wasn't his fault; he'd stopped in a queue of traffic, but the guy behind him was texting instead of paying attention to the road and didn't brake in time. Dad ended up with what he told me was a minor case of whiplash.'

'Except it wasn't,' Sam guessed, knowing that codeine wasn't the kind of painkiller prescribed for minor pain.

'No. He had horrendous backache, and the only thing that stopped the pain was codeine. The hospital prescribed them for two weeks, and assumed that Dad—being a doctor himself—would know how to taper them off properly.' Angelo grimaced. 'Of course he knew what he was supposed to do. Except he was still in pain, and nothing else he tried came close to helping. Hot and cold compresses, physio, a TENS machine—' a transcutaneous electrical nerve stimulation machine that sent little electric impulses to the affected area, to help block the pain signals going to the brain, and which several of their mums used during labour '—and he even went to a psychologist for cognitive behavioural therapy, to try and help himself think differently about the pain and try to manage it better. But the only thing that took the edge off and helped him to function normally was codeine. So he kept taking it. Without it, the pain stopped him sleeping, and he was worried that he'd make a mistake at work and end up prescribing the wrong drug or the wrong dosage for a patient.'

Broken sleep was incredibly debilitating; the worse you slept, the harder it was to manage a difficult medical condition. Angelo's dad had clearly been trapped in a vicious circle.

'Your poor dad,' she said. 'He must've been desperate.' Just as Dominic had been. His friends at work had all taken cocaine at the weekends; the drug had given him an edge he'd felt he'd needed to keep up on the trading floor at work, so he'd started taking it during the week as well. When it affected his judgement at work and he was sacked for gross misconduct, the truth about Dominic's addiction had come to light; Sam had taken her little brother to rehab and helped him try to put his life back together. Except he'd relapsed again and again and again. Told lie after lie after lie, broken promise after promise after promise.

'Addiction's hard—for the addict and for their families,' she said. 'You know what happened with my brother. You know I wouldn't have judged your dad. Why didn't you let me help?'

'Precisely because I knew what happened with your brother,' he said. 'How you took him to rehab. How you let him stay with you so you could support him. How he lied to you and stole from you and went back on the coke. You spent two years trying to get him clean, never giving up on him even when he relapsed. And then…'

He didn't say it, clearly trying to spare her feelings, but they both knew. Dominic had accidentally overdosed. And Sam had found him too late, lying on her bathroom floor. She hadn't been able to bear living in her flat, after that.

'It broke you, Sam,' he said softly. 'I met you six months later. I knew how badly it had hurt you. How could I drag you back into that kind of situation and bring all those memories back?' He swallowed hard. 'And it wasn't just the addiction.'

'How do you mean?'

'Dad started prescribing codeine for himself.'

Oh, no. Self-prescribing was seriously against

the rules, and doing it could get a doctor struck off the medical register.

'He knew you're not supposed to do it unless there's nobody else who can assess you and prescribe something for you, and either it's an emergency or it's to avoid serious deterioration in health. And you're supposed to keep a clear record stating exactly what you prescribed and why,' Angelo said.

It sounded as if his dad hadn't done any of that.

'One night, the pain was so bad, he prescribed codeine for himself. And he didn't make the proper notes. He knew what he'd done was wrong, so he covered it up.' Angelo dragged in a breath. 'He only meant to do it once. But the pain just wouldn't go away. And he knew if he asked he wouldn't get the prescriptions. So he kept going.'

'How long did he take codeine?'

'Two and a half years,' Angelo said dryly.

'What?' Sam's face was filled with shock. 'But codeine's prescription only. Surely someone must've noticed at the practice, or at the pharmacy where he got the prescriptions filled. They would've kept records and seen that the prescriptions were going on for much longer than doctors usually prescribe codeine.'

'He used online pharmacies at first,' Angelo said. 'There was a loophole in the law, so he could refuse permission for them to access his medical records, and also make the pharmacy withhold the information from his doctor about his online purchases.'

Sam frowned. 'But pharmacists know you're not supposed to take opiates for more than a week, and then it needs tapering off. And if someone's had a lot of prescriptions filled for codeine, it's pretty obvious they have a problem. How did he get away with it?'

'He only asked for a week's supply at a time, to avoid arousing suspicions. There are a lot of online pharmacies that he could cycle round, and they don't share data,' Angelo said grimly.

'Why didn't he go back to his doctor and ask for a referral to a pain clinic?'

'He did. There was a waiting list,' Angelo said. 'A really, really long one. Obviously Dad was prepared to pay for a private appointment, but the clinic he went to wasn't that helpful. He asked about an epidural steroid injection for the nerves around the painful area, but they said it wouldn't work for him.'

'That's rough,' Sam said.

'He tried to find another way. But, the longer he was on codeine, the more his tolerance grew, and the more he needed to take to deal with the pain. He never put any of his patients at risk, but he needed to find a way of managing the pain so he could function.' Angelo spread his hands. 'And he chose the wrong way. I feel horrible that I didn't have a clue about it. I mean, I rang him every week. He always seemed fine on video calls. When he wouldn't come to London, I assumed it was something to do with London having too many memories of Mum and he couldn't handle it.'

Angelo's mum had been an English doctor who'd trained in London; Angelo had followed in her footsteps and trained at her old medical school. Sam knew that his mother had died from breast cancer in his Finals year, and he'd almost chosen oncology as his specialism in his mum's memory, but during his rotations he'd fallen in love with working on the maternity unit and seeing the wonder of new lives.

'I couldn't pin my dad down to a time when I could take you to meet him in Rome. I assumed he was being cagey because he'd finally started dating someone and didn't want to say anything in case it didn't work out.' He shook his head. 'I just wish I'd realised he was hiding something a lot more serious.'

'How did you find out what was happening?'

'One of his self-prescriptions came to light during an audit,' Angelo said. 'The senior partner at his surgery investigated the issue, and made him retire on grounds of ill health. They weren't trying to dump him; they were trying to avoid him being struck off for self-prescribing, because they knew then he'd feel even worse about the situation. Though retiring really didn't help; without working as a doctor, Dad felt he didn't have anything left in his life. His colleagues tried to help him with the back pain, but nothing worked. He refused to go to rehab, and his mood got lower and lower.' He sighed. 'Dad never dated again after Mum died, so he didn't have a partner to step in and hold his hand through it, either. His brother—my Uncle Salvatore—knew something was wrong. Eventually he persuaded Dad to tell him what was going on; he didn't know how to deal with it, so he talked to me. Obviously in London I was too far away to be of much help.'

Now Sam understood why Angelo had gone straight back to Rome. 'So that was the family business you mentioned.'

He nodded. 'I wanted to get Dad into rehab so they could wean him off the codeine. Once he was out again, I wanted to be there to support him, and help him get that back pain sorted out properly. I needed to put him first.'

'I understand that, I truly do,' Sam said, 'but why didn't you just tell me the truth?'

'I was worried sick, I wasn't thinking straight, and I felt so guilty for not realising it.'

She understood that, too; she'd felt guilty for not being able to help her brother.

'All I could focus on was the fact my dad was in a lot of pain, he'd kept everything to himself instead of letting me or my uncle help him, and he'd resorted to self-prescribing codeine,' Angelo continued. 'As a doctor, he knew the risks of addiction, and he knew that taking codeine long-term could cause problems—everything from mild confusion through to severe respiratory depression. But he still did it, because for him putting up with the pain was harder than dealing with the possible risks. And all I could think of was, what if he just stopped breathing in the night because he was taking such high doses of codeine?'

'I would've been there for you, if I'd known about it, just as you were there for me,' she said quietly. 'I would've supported you. *Both* of you.'

Angelo nodded. 'I'm sorry. I know you wouldn't have judged my dad. But losing Dominic almost broke you. I didn't want to bring back all the bad memories. The only way I could think of to protect you was to push you away. That's why I said what I did. I'm sorry I hurt you, and I'm sorry I lied.' He bit his lip. 'I did the wrong thing. I know that.'

She thought about it.

Angelo had wanted to protect her, and he'd wanted to help his dad. She could understand that. But the way he'd gone about it… 'I loved you so much, Angelo. I was devastated when you dumped me. I thought we had a future together. When we went to Venice, I almost asked you to marry me.'

'I thought about proposing to you in Venice, too,' Angelo said. 'But I was planning to take you to Rome in the summer, to meet Dad and the rest of my Italian family. And then I was going to whisk you off to this amazing garden of orange trees and ask you to marry me.' He shook his head. 'But how could I drag you into what was happening in Rome? You deserved better than that.'

'I deserved better than you saying it wasn't working out and you didn't love me.'

He winced. 'I know. And I'm sorry. It wasn't true. I really, really loved you,' he said quietly. 'When things with Dad had finally settled down, I came to London to see you. To apologise, to tell you the truth about why I went away, and to ask you to give me another chance.'

'When?' She frowned. 'Until I came to Florence, I hadn't seen you for two years.'

'Because I didn't go through with it,' he said. 'The day I came back to London, there was a new receptionist on our ward, someone I didn't know. I asked her if you were on duty, and she said you'd gone away with your boyfriend Greg for the weekend and it was getting serious.'

So *that* was how he'd known.

'I wanted you to be happy,' he said, 'so I didn't want to get in your way. I came back to Rome without seeing you.

'Ironically, that was the weekend I broke up with Greg,' she said. 'He wanted to get serious—and I didn't. I knew I wasn't being fair to him. So we agreed to be friends. He's dating someone seriously now, and I really hope she gives him everything I couldn't.'

'That was how I thought, when I heard you were dating someone,' Angelo said. 'And I've barely dated, too. That first year in Rome, I was focused on Dad. I took a year out to support him, and then I went back to my training. I was too busy for relationships, between work and keeping an eye on Dad. Though he got a bit fed up with me being under his feet all the time, and he was the one who persuaded me to take the post here.' He shrugged. 'I wasn't sure at first, even though I wanted the job; I didn't want to leave him. But he pointed out that he was a lot better, he needed to stand on his own two feet, and it's quicker to get to Rome from Florence than it is from London.' He smiled wryly. 'And he said I needed to get a life. So I gave in and took the job.'

'How often do you see him now?'

'Every fortnight,' Angelo said. 'And I call him every other day in between.' He sighed. 'I'm in Rome tomorrow. I'm supposed to send him a selfie to prove that I'm dating someone.'

Sam raised her eyebrows. 'Why?'

'Because he worries about me as much as I worry about him. Because he wants a visit from his son, not a doctor who's checking him all the time for signs of a relapse. When I saw him a fortnight ago, he kept scratching his arm.' He winced. 'And, yeah, my first thought was itching and codeine. I didn't say it, but it must've shown on my face and he called me on it. It was an insect bite, not a skin reaction to codeine. I felt so ashamed; I should've trusted him instead of jumping to conclusions.'

'I was the same with Dommy,' Sam said. 'And your dad's right. You do need to see him as your dad, not as a patient. Otherwise it's going to drive you apart.'

Angelo grimaced. 'I know. But how do I stop worrying about him?'

'It's hard,' she said. 'I sometimes think if I'd made Dommy feel that I really trusted him, it might've taken off some of the pressure and helped him stay away from the coke. I think you just have take a leap of faith. Has your dad taken codeine—or anything similar—since he came out of rehab?'

'No,' Angelo said.

'You know how much hard work it is, recovering from an addiction. Why would he throw it all away, knowing he'd have to go through it all over again?'

'I guess,' Angelo said.

'Plus you supported him through it last time. So if he gets to the point where he's not managing as well as before, he'll talk to you about it instead of trying to hide it, because he knows you understand the situation and he trusts you to help him,' Sam pointed out.

Angelo thought about it. 'You're right. The irony is, he doesn't even take paracetamol, let alone anything stronger.'

'So how has he managed his back pain?'

'It turned out that the clinic he went to got it wrong. He saw another specialist, who recommended radiofrequency ablation—and that worked,' Angelo said. 'He still misses being at the surgery, but by now he would've retired anyway, so I think he's coming to terms with it. He keeps himself busy pottering about in his garden, and he's taken up watercolour painting and baking. As he pointed out to me a fortnight ago, he lives a good life. He sees his friends, he eats well, he goes swimming three times a week, he goes to his addiction support group every week, and he has Baffi for company.'

'Baffi?'

'His cat.' Angelo wrinkled his nose. 'Though the one thing I think that's missing in his life is a relationship. Mum definitely wouldn't have wanted him to spend the rest of his life on his own. But if I nag him to start dating someone, then he'll nag me even more to do the same thing.'

'So why don't you date someone?' she asked.

'I have, from time to time.' He shrugged. 'But nobody's ever matched up to you. It's never felt the same. It's always fizzled out.'

Which was exactly the way she'd felt. 'I've changed since you knew me, Angelo,' she warned. 'Just as I'm sure you've changed.'

'I've grown up, and I think we're both older and wiser. For what it's worth, Sam, I've always regretted what I did. And I'm sorry it didn't work out with Greg. I really wanted you to be happy.' He held her gaze. 'Though there's a selfish bit of me that's glad you're single.'

Her breath caught. Was he going to suggest that they tried again?

And, if he did, should they?

It had gone so badly wrong, last time. He'd left her flat, lonely and miserable. But it sounded as if he'd been just as lonely and miserable, too.

'I know it's a big ask,' he said, 'and I won't sulk or harass you if you say no. But I've missed you, Sam. I miss *us*.'

Her heart skipped a beat. She'd missed him, too. But she needed to be sensible. 'Angelo, I'm only here on secondment for three months,' she said. 'And then I have to go back to London. I've been trying to set up a research project; the funding comes through when I get back, and I'm being promoted to consultant.' She grimaced. 'That sounds a bit boastful. What I meant is, I've worked hard and it's all finally coming together.'

'You deserve it,' he said. 'But would you consider giving me a second chance while you're here? We could see how things go. If it doesn't work, then we'll part—this time, as friends. And, if it does work, then maybe before you go back to London we can talk about it, decide together where we go from there.'

The man who'd broken her heart wanted her to give him a second chance.

If she did, would she be setting herself up for yet more heartbreak? Or could they both learn from the past and make it work, this time around?

And if it did work out…would she have to be the one to make all the sacrifices? Or would they be able to work out something that was fair for all of them?

'Let me go and make that coffee I promised you,' Angelo said. 'Then you can have a few minutes to think about it without any pressure from me.'

He disappeared into the kitchen, and Sam stared out into the distance, thinking about what he'd said.

She'd never been able to forget Angelo. The attraction was definitely still there between them. He'd explained why he broke her heart the way he did, and she understood his reasons—even if she didn't entirely agree with them.

Going back to him would be a risk.

She could say no and keep their relationship strictly professional.

Or she could say yes, and see where things took them.

She looked up as Angelo walked onto the balcony, put two mugs of coffee on the table and sat opposite her.

'Right now, I feel like a teenager who's just asked the girl of his dreams if she'll go out with him and is terrified she's going to turn him down,' he said.

'That makes two of us,' she admitted. 'Part of me's scared. If I say yes, how do I know it won't go wrong again?'

'If you'll give me another chance,' he said, 'then I'll do my very best not to make the same mistakes. I'll talk to you about things instead of being arrogant and thinking I know how to deal with everything, when I clearly don't. And I know you're strong enough to understand my situation and support me.'

'That's fair,' she said. 'And you're going to Rome to see your dad tomorrow, right?'

He nodded. 'Though, even if you do decide to give me another chance, I wouldn't expect you to come with me tomorrow. I think we need time to get used to each other again before I introduce you to Dad or the rest of my Italian family.'

'That's a good point. I'm not sure I'm ready

to meet your dad yet, either,' she admitted. 'But there is one thing.'

'What?'

'You promised him a selfie of you and a date. Do you have one?'

'No.' Angelo's cheeks tinged with colour. 'I did think about asking someone at work to pose with me, just to keep him happy, but there isn't any point in lying. So I'm just going to have to be honest with him and say I didn't manage to keep my end of our bargain.'

'Bargain?' Sam asked.

'He'll keep going to his addiction support meeting every week, as long as I start dating someone.'

She stood up and took her phone out of her pocket. 'Better keep your end of the bargain, then. Come and stand with me.'

His eyes widened. 'You're going to take a selfie of us to keep my dad happy?'

'I'm going to take a selfie of you and your new—well, sort of new—girlfriend,' she said.

He actually blushed as he came to stand beside her, and she smiled. 'You always were cute,' she said softly. 'Like those Raphael cherubs.'

'You mean the ones lurking at the bottom of the painting, looking a bit bored?'

'Looking wistful,' she corrected. 'You always stuck your hand in your hair when you were studying, and your hair's always messy by the end of the day. It's one of the things that made me fall for you.'

He smiled. 'Apparently the cherubs were based on the children of Raphael's model for the Madonna. He painted them exactly as he saw them.'

She rolled her eyes. 'Trust you to know that.'

He spread his hands. 'What can I say? I've always had nerd tendencies.'

That was something else she'd liked about him.

The only answer she had was to reach up and touch her mouth to his.

He wrapped his arms round her and kissed her all the way back.

She'd forgotten how it felt to kiss Angelo: the warmth, the sweetness, the coil of desire in her stomach that tightened and grew hotter.

When he finally broke the kiss, Sam's head was spinning and Angelo looked dazed.

'Sam.'

'I know.' She traced his lower lip with the tip of her finger. 'Me, too.'

He laid his palm against her cheek. 'I can't think straight. Right now, I want to pick you up and carry you to my bed. At the same time,

I don't want to rush you. We've both changed over the years, and I want to give us time to get to know each other again. And in any case,' he admitted, 'I don't actually have any condoms.'

'Me neither.'

He gave her a wry smile. 'So now you know I wasn't planning anything. I really, honestly, just meant to cook you dinner and be there as a friend. Except I don't...' He brushed his mouth lightly against hers.

He didn't need to finish the sentence. She felt exactly the same way: that they weren't friends. They'd been lovers, knew each other intimately. And it would be oh, so easy to fall for each other again.

'Sit with me for a while?' he asked.

'It'd be a shame to waste that coffee,' she said lightly.

He smiled, moved one of the chairs away from the table, then sat down, scooping her onto his lap and wrapping his arms round her waist.

She rested her head against his shoulder. 'It's years since I sat like this with anyone.'

'Me, too,' he said.

'That photo for your dad—we still haven't taken it.' She cuddled into him and tilted her phone screen. 'Smile.' She took the snap. 'I'll message this to you later.'

'Thank you.' He twisted so he could kiss the tip of her nose. 'So we're giving it another go?'

Right now they couldn't promise each other an easy, simple future. She had a job she loved in London, and Angelo was tied to Italy because of his dad. If they were going to be together, one of them would have to make a huge sacrifice. And there were no guarantees everything would work out. 'Let's just take it one day at a time,' she said, wanting to take it cautiously.

'OK.' he said.

They sat there together until they'd finished their coffee. Then, half reluctantly, she slid off his lap. 'You've got a long journey tomorrow. I'd better go.'

'I'll walk you home,' he said.

And how different it felt, walking through Florence hand in hand with Angelo. All the colours seemed brighter, even though the sun had set. Everything seemed in sharper focus. And all around she could hear snatches of love songs.

When they reached the door to Sam's entrance hall, Angelo kissed her. 'Tomorrow evening,' he said, 'if you're not busy, maybe I can see you when I get back from Rome?'

'I'd like that,' she said.

He smiled. 'Until tomorrow evening, then.' He stole a last kiss. 'Sweet dreams.'

CHAPTER SEVEN

'GOOD TO SEE YOU, Dad.' Angelo hugged his father.

'And you.' Ruggiero returned the hug. 'Now, this time, I have my son visiting, not a doctor, right?'

'Right,' Angelo confirmed.

'Good. I thought we'd have lunch in the garden,' Ruggiero said. 'I bought cheese and tomatoes at the market yesterday, and I made bread this morning. The way your *nonna* taught me.'

'Sounds great,' Angelo said. 'I brought *cantucci*. Though they're not home-made.'

'I'm not judging. You don't have time to bake,' Ruggiero said. His eyes narrowed slightly. 'Though you look different.'

'Different how?'

'I don't know. More relaxed, perhaps. Work's going well?

'Yes.' And talking about work was a good

way of introducing the subject of Sam, Angelo thought. 'You know I told you my boss is setting up a foetal medicine unit?'

'Yes—and it sounds fascinating. It's amazing to think you can do surgery in the womb,' Ruggiero said.

'We have a professor from Paris and a specialist from London,' Angelo said. 'I have a mum on my list with triplets—a singleton, plus twins with twin-to-twin syndrome. The London specialist did laser ablation on the placenta, and I got to laser a couple of the blood vessels.'

'When I was your age, I would never have believed it possible that one day we could do *in utero* surgery,' Ruggiero marvelled.

'It felt like waving a magic wand,' Angelo said. 'We've given those babies a real chance. And it's more effective than simply draining the amniotic fluid from the recipient twin, because we've corrected the problems that caused the fluid imbalance in the first place.' He paused. 'But it's more than that. It turned out I already knew the specialist from London.'

'Someone you used to work with?'

'A bit more than that.' He smiled. 'It's Samantha.'

'What, *your* Samantha?' Ruggiero asked.

At Angelo's nod, he winced. 'That must be a bit awkward.'

'Surprisingly not, once we'd got over the shock of seeing each other again. We're both older and wiser,' Angelo said. He'd never actually told his father why he'd split up with Sam, not wanting his dad to feel he was to blame for the break-up; instead, Angelo had fudged the issue, saying instead that he and Sam had grown apart.

'So you're managing to work together without a problem?'

Angelo nodded. 'Actually, it turns out that she's still single, too.' He paused. 'We've talked about how things were in London, and while she's in Florence we're…well, seeing how things go.' He took his phone from his pocket. 'I promised you a selfie of me with my date. Here you go.'

Ruggiero studied the photograph. 'There's something about her smile that reminds me of your mum.' He looked at Angelo. 'I'm sorry I didn't meet her when you were in London. At the time, I didn't want to travel—I couldn't face having to use uncomfortable seating that would make my back worse. And I didn't want you to come to Rome, either, in case you guessed that things weren't really all right with me.'

'I assumed you were secretly dating some-one and didn't want me to know, in case I thought it was too soon,' Angelo said. 'Which, by the way, I didn't. You've been on your own for nearly a decade, Dad. Maybe it's time to meet someone.'

Ruggiero made a dismissive gesture. 'I'm not interested in dating. I could never replace your mum.'

'You wouldn't be replacing her, or dismiss-ing her memory,' Angelo said gently. 'You'd simply be opening your heart to someone new. And I can say this because I loved her, too: Mum definitely wouldn't have wanted you to be on your own. She would've wanted you to have company. Someone who loved you.'

'I'm fine as I am,' Ruggiero said. 'Now, I thought we could go for a walk before lunch.'

In other words, he didn't want to discuss it. But hopefully, Angelo thought, he'd planted a tiny seed in his dad's head. 'A walk sounds great,' he said with a smile.

It was the most relaxed day he'd spent with his father since he'd come home to Italy two years ago. They talked easily, and Angelo didn't find himself checking surreptitiously for signs that his father might have relapsed. Maybe he had Sam to thank for that; she'd made him think differently, and make the effort to trust his dad.

On his way back from Rome, he texted her from the train.

How do you fancy cocktails this evening and maybe a bit of dancing?

Her reply came back.
Sounds good. What time?

Meet you at your place, about eight?

I'll be ready. How was your dad?

Fine. And thank you for making me see him differently. Today's been a lot better. x.

There was a pause, and then YVW followed by a heart.

He couldn't help smiling.

If anything, Sam had become sweeter with age. He liked the woman she'd become. And he really, really hoped that they'd find a way for this thing between them to work.

Sam had brought only one suitcase with her to Florence: work outfits, jeans, and casual tops. She didn't have a dress, or anything remotely

suitable for going out dancing and for cocktails. And now she had roughly an hour until
the shops closed. Would that be long enough
to find a dress and shoes she could dance in
but that looked stylish as well?

She checked the internet to find out where
the clothes shops were, and called Nina on her
way out. 'Are you around, for the next hour?'

'While your goddaughter's napping, yes,'
Nina said. 'Why?'

'Because I need your fabulous fashion sense.'

Nina laughed. 'What, matching spots of
baby dribble on each shoulder?'

Sam laughed back. 'Not quite. I didn't pack
a dress, and I'm going dancing tonight, so I
need shoes and a dress, and the shops close
in an hour, and...'

'Stop panicking and breathe,' Nina cut in. 'I
take it you're going on a work night out, and
you forgot about it until the last minute?'

'Not exactly,' Sam hedged.

'Don't tell me you're going on an actual
date?'

'Um, yes. Cocktails and dancing.'

'That sounds fun,' Nina said. 'So tell me
about your date. I'm assuming he's someone
you work with? What's his name? What's he
like?'

Sam squirmed. 'You already know him. It's Angelo.'

'Angelo?' Nina sounded shocked. 'Are you sure dating him is a good idea, Sam?'

'We're just seeing how things go,' Sam said. 'Keeping everything low-key.'

'He broke your heart, last time.'

'I know, but we talked last night. I mean *really* talked. I understand why he walked away, now.'

'So he had a good reason?'

'It's complicated,' Sam hedged. 'And it's not really my place to talk about it. Let's just say it was a family thing, and I understand now.'

'Right.' Nina didn't sound in the slightest bit convinced.

'He came back for me, Nina. I had no idea. The receptionist in our old department told him I was away for the weekend with Greg. Angelo wanted me to be happy, so he walked away.' She sighed. 'How ironic is it that *that* was the weekend we broke up?'

'I just don't want you to get hurt again,' Nina said.

'I won't get hurt. Angelo's changed, and so have I.'

'Hmm. I'm reserving judgement,' Nina said. 'But, in the meantime, you need a dress and shoes. Something you can dance in. Is Florence really fashionable?'

'It's Italy,' Sam said dryly. 'Everyone looks like a model.'

'OK. Play it safe. Go for a little classic black dress, and black court shoes that are high enough to make your legs long but won't give you blisters for work. Did you take any jewellery with you?'

'Uh,' Sam said. 'Do I need jewellery?'

'Yes. Get the dress and shoes, then head for an accessory shop. You'll need a bag as well,' Nina said. 'Honestly. The first time my best friend buys a dress in *years*, and she has to do it hundreds of miles away instead of letting me have the fun of bossing her about on a shopping trip.'

'I was planning on taking photographs in the mirror and sending them to you,' Sam said. 'It's the next best thing.'

'I'll hold you to that,' Nina said.

Fifty-six minutes later—having tried on eight little black dresses and ended up going back to the very first one she'd seen—Sam was in possession of a dress, a wrap, shoes, a bag and a chunky necklace.

'Video call me when you've done your hair

and make-up,' Nina said. 'And eat carbs, if you're drinking cocktails.'

'To line my stomach. I know,' Sam said. 'Call you in a bit.'

She texted Angelo just to double-check that they weren't eating, then went to the little pizzeria round the corner to grab something to take away. Once she'd showered, done her hair and make-up and finished dressing, she video called Nina, balanced her phone on the windowsill and did a twirl so Nina could see her outfit.

'Gorgeous,' was her best friend's verdict.

'I feel ridiculously nervous,' Sam said. 'It's like being seventeen again.'

'Have fun—but maybe don't let your heart get involved, this time,' Nina advised.

'Got it,' Sam said. But the butterflies in her stomach had turned into a stampede of ostriches by the time her doorbell rang.

'Coming down,' she called into the intercom, hoping her nervousness didn't show in her voice. This was crazy. She *knew* Angelo. They'd dated for two years. They'd been at the point of settling down together. OK, so it had gone wrong, but now she understood that it hadn't been because of anything lacking in her. It had been circumstances outside both their control.

She draped the light wrap round her shoulders, locked the door and went down to meet him.

Angelo was waiting for her in the street; he looked incredibly stylish in dark formal trousers and a jacket, a pale formal shirt and highly polished shoes.

'Hi.' He looked at her and smiled, and her heart skipped a beat. 'You look lovely.'

'So do you,' she said, feeling ridiculously shy. 'How was your dad?'

'Good.' He smiled. 'I did what you said and tried to make him feel I trust him. And we had a really nice day together.'

'I'm glad,' she said, meaning it,

'Ready for cocktails?' he asked.

'Yes,' she fibbed.

He took her hand and they strolled through the cobbled streets, heading towards the river. For a moment, she wondered whether he was planning to take her to watch the sun setting from one of the bridges; the sky was washed with peach and pink as the sun neared setting point, and the reflections in the river would look amazing. But then he ushered her through an unobtrusive doorway into a reception area.

He glanced at her shoes. 'Lift, I think. Save your feet for dancing.'

The lift was small, only big enough for two

people. Standing this close to him, she could smell the woody scent of his aftershave, and it sent a shiver of desire down her spine.

'Samantha.' He rested his hands lightly on her waist and looked her in the eye.

Two years ago, he would've kissed her. Would he kiss her now?

He leaned forward, and every nerve-end tingled.

His lips brushed just below her ear. 'Whatever just put that look in your eyes, hold on to that thought.'

'I was thinking about kissing,' she said, her voice husky with need. Right now, she really, really wanted him to kiss her.

'That's what I'm thinking, too,' he said, drawing her a tiny bit closer. His mouth skimmed the curve of her neck, and she closed her eyes, but then a ping signalled that the lift doors were about to open. 'Hold that thought for later, *carissima*.'

She was glad that Angelo was holding her hand as they left the lift, because her knees felt decidedly wobbly. It was nothing to do with the height of her heels, and everything to do with the fact that he was going to kiss her later.

He led her round the corner and through another doorway, and to her delight she realised they were on a rooftop garden with a panoramic view of the city. Although they didn't have a view of the river, they could still see the sunset and the iconic buildings of Florence rising above the terracotta rooftops.

'This is gorgeous,' she said.

'I thought we'd start with drinks here, while the sun's setting,' he said, 'then move on to the dancing.'

'Sounds perfect,' she said with a smile.

'What can I get you to drink?' he asked as they reached the bar.

'I don't know.' She smiled at the barman. 'What would you recommend as the most typical drink in Florence?'

'If you'd like a cocktail, then it has to be a Negroni,' the barman said. 'It was invented in Florence a hundred years ago.'

'What's in it?' Sam asked.

'Bitters, red vermouth and gin,' the barman said. 'Or, if you'd like something a little lighter, you could try a negroni *sbagliato*, where you swap the gin for Prosecco.'

'I think I'd like the lighter version, please,' she said with a smile.

'And I'll have a traditional negroni, please,' Angelo said.

The barman mixed their drinks expertly, adding ice and a slice of blood orange to each glass. 'Enjoy,' he said.

'Thank you,' Angelo said, and walked back out to the terrace, still holding Sam's hand. 'Where would you like to sit?'

'Where we can see the Duomo, please,' she said. 'I love that building.'

'Maybe I can get tickets for us to go up inside it one day after work,' he said.

'But haven't you already done that?'

'It's worth repeating.' He found them a table, then lifted his glass in a toast. *'Salute.'*

'Cheers,' she said, lifting her own glass.

He took a sip of his drink and grimaced.

'Not great?' she asked.

'I think it's more that I'm not really much of a cocktail person. I'll order a glass of red wine, next time,' he said. 'How's yours?'

'Lovely,' she said. 'Try a sip. Bubbles make everything better.'

'Even if they're terrifyingly sweet Bellinis.' He rolled his eyes. 'Do you remember that evening we drank Bellinis in Venice?'

'In St Mark's Square, sitting outdoors by the heater because it was February, but it wasn't raining and we wanted to look up at the stars. And then dancing in the square.'

'We were the only ones dancing,' he said softly.

And it hadn't mattered. It had felt like the most romantic place in the world: just them

and the music and the stars and the wide, wide
square, back in the days when they'd definitely
been in love with each other.

Yet, two months later, it had all fallen apart.

This time round, would it work out? Or
would something else get in the way of their
happiness? She shivered.

'Cold?' he asked, moving to shrug off his
jacket.

'No, I'm fine.' She looked at him. 'Venice
was a long time ago.'

'When we were different people,' he said.
'So let's focus on the here and now.'

'Agreed,' she said.

When they'd finished their drinks, Sam insisted on buying the next round: chianti for
Angelo, and another negroni *sbagliato* for
her. Then they headed for the other side of
the river.

'I haven't actually been here before,' Angelo
said as they reached another unobtrusive doorway, 'but it's got good reviews. We're going
retro.'

Once they'd checked in his jacket and her
wrap, Sam was delighted to discover that the
club was playing music that reminded her
of her student years—including the kind of
line-dance songs that had everyone joining in.
'I'd forgotten how much I enjoyed this sort of

thing,' she said, when they'd taken a break to get some water.

'I've forgotten most of the moves,' Angelo said ruefully. 'But I agree; it's fun.'

They danced for the next hour, but then the DJ slowed everything down and Angelo drew her closer.

Sam closed her eyes, enjoying the feel of their arms wrapped round each other as they swayed to the music. Everything and everyone else in the room melted away; all she was aware of was the beat of Angelo's heart, the way the blood pulsed through her veins in exactly the same rhythm as his.

His cheek was against hers; she couldn't resist turning her head slightly and pressing a kiss to the corner of his mouth. His arms tightened round her, and he twisted so he could brush his mouth against hers.

The next thing she knew, he was really kissing her, and the long years of loneliness melted away. This was Angelo's touch, Angelo's kiss, Angelo's body heat. The man she'd loved and lost, and had somehow found again...

When someone accidentally bumped into them, apologising, he broke the kiss. Sam was hideously embarrassed to realise that the music had changed tempo, and they'd both been so lost in kissing each other that they hadn't noticed everyone else was jumping around the dance floor.

Angelo took her hand and drew her off the dance floor.

'I can't believe we just did that,' Sam said, her face heating. 'As if we're seventeen.'

'Blame it on the music,' he said, his eyes glittering with amusement. 'I don't know about you, but everything they played reminded me of our student days.' He laughed. 'No wonder we've both dropped a decade and a half off our age.'

She smiled back at him. It wasn't the music at all, she knew; it was his nearness. But she appreciated the way he'd managed to keep things light. 'Shall we find somewhere a bit quieter?'

'Sounds good to me,' he said.

When they'd collected their things, they walked back through the narrow cobbled streets to the bridge, crossed back into the old town, and strolled through the centre of Florence with their arms wrapped round each other.

Eventually, they ended up outside the entrance to Sam's building.

'Would you like to come up for coffee?' she asked.

'Yes—but I'm not going to,' he said.

She frowned. 'Why?'

'Given that we kissed each other stupid in a crowded nightclub, not noticing that the music had changed,' he said softly, 'it's obvious what will happen if we're somewhere more private. And I don't want to rush you or take you for granted. I want us both to be sure about where this is heading, first.' He stole a kiss. 'I'd like to date you again, Sam. Do things properly. Are you busy tomorrow?'

'I'd planned a hot date with a washing machine and a vacuum cleaner,' she said.

He smiled. 'Maybe you could take a rain check? The weather's meant to be nice tomorrow. I thought it might be nice to go for a drive, so I can show you some of the countryside around Florence.'

'You mean, the Roman half of you has found a ruined temple or something you want to explore,' she said drily.

'Now you mention it, there's this amphitheatre...' He laughed. 'Though we can go and see something else, if you'd rather.'

'Actually, I used to enjoy going to see your Roman ruins,' she said. 'Though even *you* couldn't find Roman ruins in Venice.'

He rubbed his cheek. 'Ah. I hate to tell you this, Sam...'

'No *way*,' she scoffed. 'The earliest bit of Venice is that church we saw at Torcello.'

'Back then, yes. But I read an article, a couple of months ago,' he said. 'Apparently, the sea level was a couple of metres lower in Roman times, so bits that are submerged now were accessible by land back then. Archaeologists have found evidence of a Roman road in the lagoon, along with remains of a possible dock. Obviously they're not accessible to the public, but the point is there really are Roman remains in Venice.'

She smiled. 'It always surprised me that you never became an archaeologist.'

'I did think about it, when I was about twelve,' he admitted. 'But, with both my parents being doctors, medicine was the obvious career choice.' He stole a kiss. 'I promise you lunch to make up for dragging you round the Roman stuff. And in the afternoon we can have a stroll round a garden. One with wisteria.'

'I'd really like that,' she said. 'I'll walk over to you. What time?'

'Nine?' he suggested.

'I'll be there,' she promised.

'Good.' He kissed her. 'See you tomorrow. Remember a hat––and not one that can blow away easily.'

The next morning, Sam woke with a smile on her face. A whole day with Angelo, exploring the hills around Florence. Remembering days they'd spent like this in the past, she dressed for walking, grabbed a quick coffee and some toast, filled a water bottle and put it in her bag, then headed over to his flat and rang his intercom.

'Dr Clarke, reporting for duty to explore ancient ruins,' she teased.

He laughed. 'I'll be right down.'

His car turned out to be low-slung and sleek and red, with a soft top; now she realised why he'd been so specific about the hat not blowing away easily. She felt like a million dollars as he drove them through Florence and out to the hills. Italy in the summer, in a soft-top car and with the sun shining: it didn't get any better than this.

'So where are we going?' she asked.

'Fiesole—though I'm taking the long way round, as it's a pretty drive and I think you'll enjoy it,' he said.

The countryside was gorgeous, all rolling hills and patchwork fields and cypress trees. Sam couldn't resist taking snaps as they drove along. Fiesole turned out to be a very pretty town, its main square lined with little cafés as well as being a backdrop for the cathedral and its bell tower.

They explored the ruined Roman baths with

their stone arcades and the amphitheatre, marvelling over how much had been preserved.

'Stand here by the arcade,' Angelo said. 'You've got the bell tower in the background, too—that'll make a nice photo for your mum. I'll take it on my phone and send it over to you.'

When they'd had their fill of the ruins, they walked up the steep, narrow street to the priory. At the top, they could see the hillside sloping down to olive groves and a line of cypresses, and then Florence rising up in the distance with the Duomo clearly visible in the centre.

'That's just stunning,' Sam said. 'Thank you for bringing me here.'

'My pleasure.' He stole a kiss. 'I hoped you'd like it here. And it's good just to spend time with you.'

After lunch in the town square, Angelo drove them to a villa with formal gardens; to Sam's delight, there was a wisteria in full bloom, and she insisted on taking photographs of them together next to it. The gardens were beautiful, full of box hedges and fountains and geraniums spilling out of terracotta pots; the formal terracing led to a perfectly turquoise lake. Even in the heat of the afternoon sun, the gardens felt deliciously cool, and Sam enjoyed the fact that Angelo kissed her in every single secluded corner.

She enjoyed a drive through the hills; the scenery was spectacular, and made her fall in love with Italy all over again.

She gave Angelo a sidelong glance. It would be easy to fall in love with him all over again, too. The day they'd spent together reminded her of so many days out they'd had before. They liked the same things, saw the world the same way.

But, even though she understood now why he'd walked away from her, she couldn't quite let herself relax fully with him. How could she be sure that he wouldn't shut her out again, the next time life threw him a curveball? If she trusted him with her heart, would he break it all over again?

Spending today with Sam made Angelo realise how much he'd missed her. How much he'd missed *them*.

But he knew he needed to give her time. If he rushed her now, she'd back away. They needed to get to know each other again, and she needed to learn to trust him.

Would the few weeks she had in Italy be enough for them to sort things out between them? Maybe he needed to take the leap of faith with that, too.

He parked the car, and smiled at Sam. 'I guess I'd better walk you back to your hot date with the laundry.'

She wrinkled her nose. 'The laundry won't mind waiting, and I don't want today to end just yet. Can I take you to dinner?'

He didn't want today to end, either. 'Thank you. I'd love that.'

So he found himself walking hand in hand with her across the Ponte Vecchio to Oltrarno. Past the padlocks inscribed with lovers' initials attached to the railing, past the jewellery shops, through the narrow streets lined with workshops making everything from violins to mosaics to shoes, and finally they found a tiny restaurant with a barrel-vaulted brick roof, red-and-white-checked cloths on the tables, and a chalk board stating the day's menu.

Sam gazed through the window. 'I've seen plenty of restaurants with wine bottles used as a candle-holder, but never as lampshades for the overhead lights. This is so pretty. Can we eat here?'

'Sure,' he said.

They ordered tortellini, followed by chicken stuffed with Gorgonzola and wrapped in

Parma ham, and the waiter brought them a jug of Chianti.

'I need to find one of these for Nina,' Sam said, admiring the deep blue pottery jug with its white daisies. 'This'd be perfect on her kitchen windowsill, full of flowers.'

'How is Nina?' Angelo asked. He'd always liked Sam's best friend.

'Fine. Since you last saw her, she got married and had a baby. Lily, my goddaughter, is the most amazing baby in the world,' Sam said with a smile.

Was that a hint of wistfulness in her eyes? Angelo wondered. Did Sam want children? They'd never really had a serious discussion about children, but he'd assumed that eventually they'd have a family together.

'Hang on—you can see for yourself,' she said, and fished her phone from her bag. She flicked into the photo app and brought up an album entitled 'Lily', then passed the phone to him.

It started with pictures of Sam sitting on Nina's hospital bed, cuddling a tiny baby. As he scrolled through the photos, he could see Sam as a proud godmother holding the baby in a christening gown, and he could see Lily growing and changing before his eyes, rolling over, sitting up, crawling, and finally pulling herself up onto the furniture with a look of mingled glee and satisfaction.

'That one was a couple of days before I came to Florence,' Sam said. 'She's cruising, now. And I have to admit that's the thing I'm missing most, over here: the fact I won't be there for when Lily starts walking all on her own,' she said ruefully. 'Though Nina's promised to send me a video. She sent me that one yesterday of Lily waving to me.'

Angelo watched it, then handed the phone back. 'She looks adorable.'

'She is.' The wistfulness was back in Sam's expression, but vanished as the waiter came over with their tortellini.

He kept the conversation light during dinner, then held her hand all the way back to her flat. He'd intended to just kiss her goodnight on the doorstep, but then she said, 'Come up for coffee.'

How could he resist?

'That's an amazing fresco,' he said when she showed him into the living room.

'Isn't it just? I can't get over how there's so much gorgeous art everywhere you look in Florence.'

'It's pretty spectacular,' he agreed.

'Better than Rome?' she teased as she started making coffee.

'Rome has more fountains than Florence,' he said. 'Not to mention the Pantheon.'

'Didn't I read somewhere that it's slightly smaller than the Duomo?'

'Very slightly,' he admitted. 'But Rome has the Colosseum.'

'Yeah, but Florence is all Michelangelo.'

He coughed. 'Sistine Chapel, anyone?'

She laughed. 'I love it when you go all pompous about Rome. And you just annexed the Vatican as Roman.'

Angelo laughed back. 'That's Dad's influence. Everywhere leads back to Rome. But, growing up in Rome, with all the ruins mixed in with new buildings, it's as if you can blink and go back two thousand years. It's always fascinated me.'

'Dad's the same. I think if you ever went to Pompeii together, Mum and I would have to leave you both there for a week.'

'That might *just* be long enough,' he teased back.

He honestly meant to just have coffee and leave. But the only place to sit was next to Sam, on the sofa. He ended up with his arm round her, and that led to kissing—until he was almost dizzy with need.

This had to stop.

While he still could.

He broke the kiss and stroked her face. 'I'm trying really hard not to rush you. So I'm going now. But thank you for spending today with me. It's been perfect.'

She brushed her mouth lightly against his, and every nerve-end she'd touched tingled.

'I enjoyed it, too,' she said. 'Tuscany's gorgeous.' She held his gaze. 'So are you.'

It felt as if all the air had just emptied out of his lungs, and he couldn't speak.

Crazy. They'd been apart for longer than they'd been together. But he'd never been able to forget her. Never stopped missing her.

But if he rushed her now, he was scared she'd end up regretting it. Regretting him. Regretting their second chance.

'Sam. I'd better go,' he said softly. 'I'll see you at work tomorrow.' Reluctantly, missing her warmth the moment he moved away from her, he got to his feet.

She, too, stood up. And her kiss goodbye at her front door made his blood feel as if it were fizzing all the way back to his own flat.

Taking it slowly was going to drive him insane. But if it meant he'd get her back for good, he'd do it.

CHAPTER EIGHT

BACK ON THE WARD, Sam and Angelo treated each other strictly as colleagues, and if they had lunch together it was always as part of a group. They worked together on the more complicated cases on Angelo's list, and Sam was busy teaching new procedures to a group of medics that didn't always include Angelo.

As part of taking their new relationship slowly, they'd agreed not to see each other every evening. On Tuesday, Sam went to an aerobics class with some of the midwives and out for a healthy dinner with them afterwards. On Thursday, she and Angelo were both on an early shift; after work, he took her to the Bardini Gardens. She was utterly charmed by the long flight of baroque steps in the centre of the garden, which led to a terrace with stunning views over the city. But her absolute favourite part of the garden was the bit Angelo told her he'd saved until last: the wisteria tunnel.

The sweet, musky scent, the gorgeous purple of the flowers cascading down like a water-fall, the butterflies alighting to drink their fill of nectar...

'This is perfect,' she said.

'I knew you'd like it,' he said, looking pleased.

The week zoomed by; the following Thursday, Angelo came into the Foetal Medicine Unit to find Sam, who was in Henri's office.

'I've got a possible new case for the unit,' he said. 'And I think you're the parents' last hope, as well as mine.'

'OK. Talk us through it,' Henri said.

'Rosa Pozzoli is twenty-five weeks pregnant,' Angelo said. 'The baby has a growth in the lung. It's a non-cancerous tumour, but it's grown since the last scan, three weeks ago, and it looks as if it's starting to squash the baby's heart. I'm worried that the baby's starting to go into heart failure.'

'Can we see the scans?' Sam asked.

'Of course. May I?' Angelo gestured to Henri's computer.

Henri vacated his seat. 'Go ahead, Angelo.'

Angelo logged in to the system, brought up two scan pictures on the screen, and huddled round the desk with Sam and Henri. 'This one's the last scan—and this is today's.'

'Your diagnosis is spot on,' Henri said. 'If we leave operating until after the birth, the baby won't make it.'

'So we need to operate now.' Sam zoomed in on the area round the tumour. 'It looks as if there's just one blood vessel feeding the tumour—or have I missed something?'

'No, I agree,' Henri said.

'If we use an interstitial laser to seal off the vessel,' Sam said, 'it should stop the tumour growing.'

'How strong is the baby?' Henri asked. 'Because we need to tell the parents there's a possibility the baby's heart might stop under the strain of the procedure.'

'The baby's weaker than I'd like. But, as you said,' Angelo reminded him, 'if we leave it, the baby will die. Cutting off the blood supply to the tumour will at least give the baby a chance.'

Henri inclined his head. 'All right. Do you want to take this one, Sam?'

'I've done something similar to this,' Sam said, 'but not a case that involves a heart. If the parents are happy for us to go ahead, then yes, I'd like the chance to do the operation— but I'd like you to be there, Henri, in case I need you to step in.'

'That's fine,' Henri said.

'Are the parents with you now, Angelo?' Sam asked.

'No. I sent them off to go and have a walk round the hospital gardens while I talked to you, to see if anything can be done. There's nothing worse than being stuck in a room, waiting and worrying about what the doctors are going to say,' he said.

'OK. Bleep me when you're ready,' she said, 'and meanwhile I'll take a closer look at these scans.'

Angelo went back to his consulting room, saw his next set of parents, and then bleeped Sam when the Pozzolis came back.

He introduced her swiftly to the Pozzolis. 'Sam, this is Rosa and Cosimo Pozzoli. Rosa and Cosimo, this is Dr Sam Clarke, a specialist in foetal medicine from London who's here with us in Florence on secondment,' he said. 'She's been looking at your scan.'

The Pozzolis both looked worried sick. 'Can you do anything to help our baby, Dr Clarke?'

'There's a blood vessel feeding the tumour. I can use a laser to seal off that blood vessel, which should mean that the tumour will stop growing,' Sam said. 'But I do need to warn you that it's an invasive procedure, which always carries a risk of miscarriage, and there's also a possibility that your baby's heart might stop during the operation.'

'But if you don't do the operation, the tumour will keep growing and the baby will die anyway,' Cosimo said. 'This is the best chance we have of her surviving.'

'We understand that there are risks,' Rosa said, 'but the operation will also give us all hope. If you can save our baby, then please— whatever it takes, do it.'

'Let me talk you through the operation before you make a decision,' Sam said. 'The thing is, when we operate on babies outside the womb, they're still. Inside the womb, they're moving in amniotic fluid. I need the baby to be as still as possible, because I have to be very exact with the laser. This means I'll need to give the baby an anaesthetic during the operation.'

Cosimo looked amazed. 'You can give an unborn baby an anaesthetic?'

Sam nodded. 'I've done it before. What we do is put the needle in the baby's bottom.'

Rosa bit her lip. 'That sounds very risky.'

Cosimo said again, 'But if we don't do anything, Rosa, the baby will die.'

'Have you done an operation like this before?' Rosa asked.

'I've done something similar,' Sam said,

'and if you choose to go ahead, I'll have Professor Henri Lefevre from Paris with me when I operate. If I have even the slightest doubt about anything, I'll refer to him.'

The Pozzolis asked a few more questions, some of which Angelo could answer, and then Rosa took Cosimo's hand. 'This is our baby's best chance. So yes, please, we'd like to go ahead.'

'I promise to take the very best care of both of you,' Sam said. 'I'll schedule you in for tomorrow morning. You'll be awake for the operation, Rosa, so you'll know exactly what's happening, though you won't feel any pain. And we should be able to give you a bonus view of your baby's face, so you have something to look forward to. I know it's hard, but try to concentrate on that rather than worrying.' She smiled. 'If you think of anything else you want to ask, write it down and we'll talk about it tomorrow. I'll leave you with Angelo for now. See you in the morning.'

After work, Angelo had booked them tickets to go inside the Duomo. He'd been before, but he enjoyed the experience—and even more than that he enjoyed seeing the amazement on Sam's face as they climbed the narrow, winding staircase inside the narrow, low-ceilinged passageway and saw the dips in the centre of the steps made by hundreds of feet before them.

'This last bit's almost vertical!' Sam whispered in horror. 'I can't believe how far apart the steps are.'

'Use the handrail to pull yourself up,' Angelo whispered back. 'I'll be behind you. I won't let you fall.'

They climbed the last few steps and then they were back in daylight, the deep blue Florentine sky above them with puffy white clouds, and could walk round the base of the lantern at the top of the dome to see the whole of the city spread out before them. From this high up, even the bell tower next to the cathedral looked small. Angelo pointed out the different churches and buildings that rose above the terracotta rooftops.

'And all those villages dotted about the hills—it's so pretty,' Sam said.

She took a selfie of them at the top, with the glorious views around them.

'Are you glad you did it—even though it's four hundred and thirty-six steps?' he asked.

'For views like this, definitely,' she said with a smile. 'And it was incredible to see the frescoes on the inside of the dome close up, too.'

Once back at the bottom of the stairs, they

looked around the cathedral, and then Angelo enjoyed showing her the peacock mosaic in the crypt. 'There's a list of names in the mosaic, showing the people who paid for the floor,' he said. 'It even says how many feet of floor space they paid for. It says the peacock was paid for by someone called Obsequentius.'

'Incredible—and it's still here, all these hundreds of years later, the colours still bright,' she marvelled.

Back outside, they bought ice creams from one of the gelateria near the cathedral, then strolled through the city centre, hand in hand.

'Thank you for distracting me,' Sam said. 'I really needed that.'

'Are you nervous about tomorrow?' he asked.

'A bit,' she admitted. 'I'm usually nervous, the night before an operation, because I'm so aware of just how tiny my patients are. There's no room for error. Even a millimetre can make the difference between success and heartbreak.' She grimaced. 'This evening feels worse than usual, though I guess it's because it's the first time I've done this particular procedure.'

'I've watched you operate,' he said, 'and you're good at what you do. Plus you said you've done something similar before. This won't be very different.'

'No.' She wrinkled her nose. 'I guess now's the right time for me to worry and fret and feel nervous, because there's no room for nerves in my operating theatre.'

'Look at the flip side,' he said. 'You're giving hope to parents who would definitely have lost their unborn children without intervention.'

She nodded, and glanced at him. 'Are you busy this evening?'

'I'm not doing anything in particular,' he said.

'I could do with a little bit more distraction,' she said. 'Tell me your worst jokes.'

'If you want terrible jokes, you really need someone from Paediatrics,' he said with a smile. 'But I can offer you an alternative. How about streaming a comedy show on the TV and a glass of wine?'

'That sounds wonderful,' she said.

Angelo took her back to his flat and set her in front of the TV with the remote control and a glass of wine. 'I'll make us something to eat,' he said.

'Anything I can do to help?' she asked.

'It's fine. Just sit and chill,' he said with a smile.

He made chicken risotto with lemony steamed green beans, which they ate on his balcony; then they curled up together on the sofa. Angelo glanced down a few minutes later and could see that Sam was almost asleep. He was tempted to ask her to stay the night, but then she'd be in a rush in the morning. It wouldn't be fair to add to the stress of the delicate operation she'd be performing.

'Hey, sleepyhead. I'll walk you home,' he said gently.

She stretched, yawned and got to her feet. 'Thank you,' she said. 'For putting up with me having a fit of doubts. I really appreciate it.'

'Any time.'

He walked her home, and kissed her goodnight on her doorstep. 'Call me if you can't sleep,' he said. 'Even if it's stupid o'clock. I'll be there.'

She kissed him back. 'Thank you. See you tomorrow.'

The next morning, Sam went for a run to shake off the last of her nerves. She showered and washed her hair, and by the time she'd walked to work she felt every inch the professional she normally was.

She had her weekly appointment to see the Bianchis with Angelo, first thing, and she was really happy with the scans; the triplets were all doing well, and the smaller twin was starting to catch up to his sibling.

She caught up with the Costas, too, in the special care unit. 'I'm due in Theatre, but I wanted to see how you were getting one,' she said.

'We're allowed to take Paola home today,' Raffaella told her, beaming.

'That's fantastic news,' Sam said, taking the opportunity for a cuddle with the baby. 'She's looking well. Did you get the scan results back?'

'Yes. She's been diagnosed with Weaver Syndrome,' Mauro said.

It was a rare genetic condition associated with rapid growth, Sam knew, and it explained why Paola's head had been so large.

'Apparently she might have very mild learning difficulties and, because her bones will develop faster than average, she might have problems with balance and co-ordination,' Raffaella said. 'But the main thing is she's with us and she's healthy, and we'll do our best to give her all the support she needs.'

'We just can't wait to get her home,' Mauro said. 'And we can't thank you enough for what you did.'

'It wasn't just me. It was the whole team,'

Sam said. 'And I'd better give this little one back, even though I could sit here and cuddle her all morning.'

When she'd taken her leave of the Costas, she checked in with Rosa and Cosimo—who were with Angelo—then went to scrub in.

'How are you doing?' Angelo asked as they headed for the scrub room.

'A lot better than yesterday,' she said. 'Thanks again for putting up with that wobble, last night.'

'You're welcome,' he said. 'And you would've done the same for me.'

She finished scrubbing in, then went into the operating theatre and talked the team through what was going to happen. Everything was ready before Rosa was wheeled in: the needle, the laser fibre, the setting of the machine.

'You're going to feel some cold antiseptic on your tummy, Rosa, and then a sharp scratch with the local anaesthetic,' she said. 'You won't feel any pain, but you might feel a little bit of pressure from time to time. Anything you're worried about, tell Angelo—and if you need me to stop, that's fine.'

'I'm OK,' Rosa said, though her eyes were wide with worry.

Once the anaesthetist had checked that Rosa

was numb, and she could see that Angelo was focused on getting Rosa to breathe slowly and calmly, Sam got to work. Guided by the scanner, she put the anaesthetic into the baby's bottom, then slid the laser fibre through the narrow metal tube.

One tiny blood vessel.

If she got this right, she'd be saving a life.

If she got it wrong...

She closed her eyes for a moment and took a deep breath, then guided the laser fibre so it was next to the blood vessel feeding the tumour.

'OK. Fire,' she said coolly.

She checked on the screen, and relief flooded through her: the blood vessel was blocked. She watched the area for a few more moments, checking that there wasn't even the tiniest leak, and was satisfied that all was well.

'All done,' she said quietly, and removed the laser.

She checked the baby's heartbeat. 'Nice and steady,' she said. 'The blood vessel that fed the tumour is blocked, so the tumour should stop growing, and the baby's heart and lungs will have space to grow and mature,' she said. 'And I promised you that you could see the baby's face, Rosa and Cosimo.' She moved the scanner head and the baby's head came into view. 'Here we go. Meet your little one.'

Cosimo's eyes were wet. 'Thank you. I can't begin...' His voice broke.

'It's all good. This is my job, and being able to make a difference is what gets me up in the mornings,' she said softly. 'Rosa, you're in for observation for the rest of today, but if all's well you can go home tomorrow. Take it easy. And I'll call in to see how you're doing, OK?'

Once she'd debriefed the team, the day sped by; she saw the rest of the patients on her list, checked in again with the Pozzolis, and went out for an aerobics class and dinner with her friends on the midwifery team.

She hadn't had a chance to see Angelo since the operation, but they'd texted to arrange going out together the next day; he'd promised to take her exploring another part of Tuscany. Sam was growing to love the area, and she could completely understand why painters were drawn to it.

But she was beginning to think that it wasn't just the beautiful countryside and architecture that made Florence feel so special. It was because Angelo was here. The more she got to know him again, the more she thought she was falling back in love with him.

On the one hand, she didn't want to rush

into things, only to find she'd made a mistake. On the other, she only had a few weeks left in Italy. At the end of her secondment, would Angelo want her to stay?

That would mean giving up the research project she'd worked so hard to set up—and her promotion. Yet if Angelo came to London with her he'd be too far from his dad.

She couldn't see a solution that would work for them both, without either of them having to give up something important. They really needed to talk about it, but for now she wanted to enjoy their summer together.

Even if it had been pouring with rain, Angelo thought, it would've felt as if the sun was shining brightly—because he was spending the whole day with Sam.

When his doorbell rang, he practically skipped down the stairs to meet her.

'Good morning.' He couldn't resist stealing a kiss.

'So where are we off to, today? Finding more Roman stuff?' she asked.

'There's a bit, yes, but it's a place that's meant to be really pretty. And it's somewhere I haven't visited yet.'

'Mystery tour, hmm?' She grinned, and stole a kiss. 'Bring it on.'

He drove them to the medieval city of Lucca; once they'd parked, he took her hand and they walked through one of the gates in the enormous brick wall surrounding the city. 'There's a walk along the top of the walls,' he said. 'I thought it might be nice to do that first, then find somewhere for coffee and pastries.'

'Sounds good to me,' she said.

A narrow passageway and some steps led them up through the defensive wall. At the top, there was a wide path, lined with trees on both sides.

'I really wasn't expecting this,' she said. 'When you said a walk along the walls, I assumed it'd be like the city walls at York, where it's quite narrow and you have to squeeze past people, but this is almost like a boulevard in Paris. I bet it's really lovely here in autumn.'

'And what a view,' he said. 'The city to one side, and the mountains to the other. I can see why Lucca is called the city of a hundred churches.'

Once they'd strolled around the walls, their arms wrapped round each other, they headed back down the steps and went into the centre of the city. They went through an archway and found themselves in an enormous oval piazza. The tall cream, white and yellow buildings followed the line of the square, and many of the doorways on the ground floor seemed to be arches, garlanded with climbing plants.

'This square used to be the site of the Roman amphitheatre,' Angelo said. 'I love how the buildings have kept the shape of it.'

There were plenty of cafés to choose from; they found a table under a parasol with a view of the square and ordered coffee and delicious-looking cinnamon pastries.

'I hope you don't mind, but I booked tickets for one place that intrigued me,' Angelo said. He glanced at his watch. 'Though we've plenty of time for coffee and looking round other bits of the city, first.'

When they'd finished their coffee, they went in search of the remains of the amphitheatre in the outer perimeter of the walls, and found thin Roman bricks in the shape of archways set into saffron-coloured stucco.

'Another one to tick off your list,' Sam teased.

They made their way through a narrow street, and then Angelo said, 'Look up.' A fourteenth-century brick tower loomed on the skyline.

'Hang on—are those *trees* on the top of that tower?' Sam asked, sounding surprised.

'Seven oak trees,' he confirmed.

'I've heard of rooftop gardens, but oak trees?'

'I looked it up. Apparently, when the Guinigi family built the tower, there were seven brothers, so it's thought that one tree was planted for each brother,' he said. 'We're right on time for our tickets, so let's go and work off those pastries.'

In the centre of the tower, they looked up to see the metal openwork stairs hugging the walls all the way to the top. 'Ready?' Angelo asked.

The climb was relentless, but finally they reached the top. The oak trees gave some shade against the heat of the sun; the terracotta rooftops of the city were spread out before them, dotted with bell towers or churches and greenery showing the gardens. In the distance, Mount Pisano loomed, and behind them they could see the huge ellipsis of the piazza where they'd had coffee.

Not far from the tower was the Roman house that had been found in the basement of a restaurant, during renovations.

'I knew there'd be something Roman,' Sam said with a grin when they stopped outside.

When they'd had their fill of the museum, they visited the cathedral to see the tomb of Ilaria del Carretto.

'Those ringlets—I've never seen such realistic carving,' Sam said. 'And that headdress with the flowers is so pretty. I can see why they call her the "sleeping beauty".'

'And the little dog at her feet,' Angelo said. 'Apparently she died in childbirth.'

'Six centuries ago.' Sam sighed. 'Nowadays, we could've saved her.'

'And you're saving babies,' Angelo said softly, 'who couldn't have been saved even ten years ago, let alone six centuries back.'

'It's a privilege,' Sam said. 'And I love what we do. I love cuddling a baby we've helped through a tough time.' She smiled. 'Even if I'm off duty, I want to be there when the Bianchi babies arrive. Three cuddles.'

'My favourite bit's the first cry,' he said. 'And when you look into a newborn's eyes and see all the wonder of the universe.'

'All the promise of the future,' she agreed. *The promise of the future.*

Angelo was really starting to hope that it might happen for them. That he and Sam could finally put his stupid mistakes behind them, and get back together for good.

Though at the same time he was aware that there were issues. He was trying hard to trust his dad not to relapse, but London was too far away for him to keep a proper eye on his dad and it wasn't fair to ask his uncle to take on the burden. And Ruggiero was adamant that he wouldn't leave Rome. Yes, he could ask Sam to stay, but that would mean she had to give up the research project she was looking forward to starting, plus she'd be turning down a promotion. It wasn't fair to ask her to make all the compromises.

He racked his brain, but for the life of him he couldn't find a fair solution.

CHAPTER NINE

OVER THE NEXT few weeks, Sam fell into a routine with Angelo; one night a week, they did something in Florence followed by having dinner together, and on one of their days off they explored Tuscany. Together, they'd made a list of places they wanted to see—everything from the famous leaning tower at Pisa, where they took pictures of each other 'holding' the tower up before climbing up the worn steps to the top, to Siena with its stunning cathedral. They drove through Chianti country and stopped to tour one of the vineyards and taste the wine, and they explored the rocky coastline, discovering a quiet beach with golden sand and clear turquoise water that was more than worth the steep climb down the steps to get to it.

With every day they spent together, Sam was finding herself falling more in love with Angelo again. Yet, at the same time, she was aware of the ticking clock. She was due back in England at the end of July. Could they make their relationship work long-distance? Or would one of them have to compromise and move to the other's country?

Or maybe she was getting ahead of herself, because he'd still kept her at the holding hands and kissing stage.

Maybe, she thought, she needed to let him know that she was ready to move their relationship forward. Not quite back to how they'd once been, because they'd both changed: but back to that old closeness.

On Wednesday evening, Angelo had done the handover and was ten minutes away from finishing organising some follow-up appointments when one Emilia, one of the junior midwives, rushed in to his office. 'Angelo, I've got a mum in birthing room three. I think the baby has shoulder dystocia. I called Lydia for help, and she's with the mum now, but she asked me to come and get you.'

Shoulder dystocia, where a baby's shoulders got stuck in the mum's pelvis during birth, was a condition that could cause serious problems for both the baby and the mum. For the baby, there was the risk of a brachial nerve injury— the nerves between the neck and shoulders—

that could cause weakness or even paralysis in the upper arm; for the mum, there was the risk of a serious tear or heavy blood loss after the birth. There was a range of manoeuvres that could help free the baby, but if they didn't work the mum would need an emergency section.

'I'm on my way now,' he said. 'Give me thirty seconds to send a text, and then fill me in on the way.' He'd had plans with Sam for a late dinner, that evening, but he wasn't going to walk out on a mum and a team who needed his help, so it was fairer to cancel now than to leave it to the last minute.

Sorry, have to cancel dinner. Baby with suspected shoulder dystocia. Call you soon as I can. xx.

As soon as the text had gone, he focused on Emilia. 'Tell me the mum's history.'

'Nicoletta's twenty-eight, forty-one weeks pregnant, and this is her second baby. Her daughter was born two years ago, and everything was normal, though the baby was quite big.'

First babies tended to be smaller than subsequent babies; she'd gone just over term with this baby, so the chances were that this baby would be bigger.

'This time round, the pregnancy's been uncomplicated—she's not diabetic and her BMI's under thirty—and all her scans have been normal. She came in very early this morning, three centimetres dilated, so the team on the shift before me encouraged her to continue walking about. Four hours later, her membranes ruptured, but she was still three centimetres dilated.'

A longer second stage, then. 'Did you give her anything to help with labour?' Angelo asked.

'The night team gave her a syntocinon infusion and we were monitoring the baby with CTG. Everything was fine when I took over as her midwife,' Emilia said. 'Four hours after the infusion, she was at seven centimetres, and four hours later, she was at ten centimetres and started pushing. When the baby's head crowned, her chin seemed to be wedged against Nicoletta's perineum. I tried delivering the baby's shoulders during the next two contractions, but it didn't happen—that's when I asked Nicoletta to stop pushing and called Lidia. She asked me to come and get you.'

'Have you come across many cases of shoulder dystocia before?' Angelo asked.

'The is the first one I've actually come across—I'd only ever seen a "turtle head" presentation on a training video before today. I know the theory,' Emilia said. 'We go through the "helperr" mnemonic.'

'Starting with calling for help, and then E for "end pushing", which you've already done,' Angelo said. 'Hopefully between us we can help Nicoletta change position and it will get the baby unstuck. In about ninety per cent of cases, the McRoberts manoeuvre does the trick.'

In the delivery suite, Lidia introduced him to Nicoletta and her partner.

'I'm sure Lidia and Emilia have explained what's happening,' he said gently, 'so what we're going to do now is try changing your position to give the baby a bit more room inside you, and that will hopefully help the baby move enough so her shoulders come unstuck and we can help you deliver her safely. We'll try each manoeuvre for thirty seconds or so, and if it doesn't release the baby's shoulders we'll move onto the next one.'

'I just want my baby to be safe,' Nicoletta said. 'Do whatever you have to.'

'Thank you,' he said.

'I've assessed Nicoletta for an episiotomy,' Lidia said, 'and I don't think it will help.'

Angelo knew how experienced the senior midwife was, and he trusted her judgement completely. 'OK,' he said, and turned to Emilia. 'First manoeuvre?'

'L,' she said. 'Legs. The McRoberts manoeuvre.'

In nearly every case Angelo had seen, it had done the trick and the baby's shoulders had come unstuck, though he had a funny feeling about this one. He couldn't put his finger on why, but every instinct told him this was going to be tricky.

'We're going to help you press your legs up with your thighs against your belly, Nicoletta,' Angelo said; together he and Lidia helped Nicoletta to flex her hips.

The baby was still stuck. He glanced at Emilia.

'P—suprapubic pressure,' the junior midwife said, and pressed on Nicoletta's lower belly just above her pubic bone; when the baby didn't move, she tried a rocking motion. She glanced at Angelo and shook her head.

Still stuck.

'Next?' Lidia asked.

'E—enter manoeuvres,' Emilia said.

'I'm going to try to rotate the baby's shoulder and help the baby's arm out of the birth canal,' Angelo told Nicoletta.

But although he'd done the procedures before, in this case they didn't work.

'R—roll onto hands and knees,' Emilia said.

But helping Nicoletta roll over onto all fours didn't release the baby's shoulder, either.

'R—refer,' Lidia finished wryly.

Which meant they needed to act fast. The big risk now was of the baby suffering from hypoxia; she needed to be delivered in the next five minutes.

'Nicoletta, the baby's really wedged,' Angelo said. 'We're going to need to give you a Caesarean section—and I'll need to push the baby's head back into your pelvis.'

He sent Emilia to get the anaesthetist and the neonatal team, gave Nicoletta medication to reduce her contractions, then rotated the baby's head and pushed it back.

Within a couple of minutes Nicoletta had been whisked into Theatre, with Lidia holding the baby's head in place while Angelo scrubbed in.

A minute later, he'd delivered the baby. As always, he was on tenterhooks until the first cry came; then he relaxed and finished sewing up Nicoletta while Lidia, Emilia and the neonatal team concentrated on the baby.

He examined Nicoletta; thankfully there was no sign of a severe tear, but he'd talk to the next shift and ask them to keep an eye on her drain and the blood loss.

'How's the baby doing?' he asked the neo-natal specialist.

'She's doing fine. Five-minute Apgar score of nine. There's some brachial nerve damage on the arm that was stuck, but that should resolve itself, and there's no sign of hypoxia.'

'That's good to know,' he said.

Once he'd debriefed the team, and Nicoletta had come round from the anaesthetic enough to cuddle her baby and for him and the neo-natal specialist to talk to her and her husband about what had happened and what it meant for the baby and any future pregnancies, he wrote up his notes and texted Sam.

Ended up in Theatre. Mum and baby both doing well. x.

The reply came back almost immediately.

Good to hear. Have leftovers here if you want dinner? x.

He wasn't that hungry, and he was tired; it had been a long day.

Tired and a bit out of sorts. Not fair to make you put up with that. x.

I don't mind out of sorts. Maybe you'll feel better if someone makes a fuss of you. x.

He couldn't help smiling. Seeing her would definitely make him feel lighter.

On my way now. x.

It didn't take long to walk to her flat and press the Entryphone buzzer. She let him up, and as she opened her front door to him he could smell something delicious.

Suddenly he realised he actually *was* that hungry, and wolfed down the chicken wrapped in Parma ham that she'd served with a simple salad.

And then then were strawberries with the most perfect vanilla ice cream.

'I bought a take-out carton from the gelateria round the corner,' she said.

'Excellent idea,' he said. 'Thank you for feeding me. I feel human again, now.'

'Shoulder dystocia where McRoberts doesn't work is scary stuff,' she said. 'I'm glad to hear the mum and baby are fine.'

'The baby has Erb's palsy,' he said. 'Edoardo thinks it will resolve in a few days, but it's still not great for those poor parents. And there were no real red flags to make any of the team think the baby would get stuck. Yes, the baby was big, but half the babies with shoulder dystocia weigh less than four kilos. It was her second pregnancy, there weren't any complications and her last birth was uncomplicated.'

'Sometimes it just happens.'

'That what I told Emilia. She's been fretting that she missed something.'

'The main thing is you delivered the baby safely,' she said.

'Yeah.' He rubbed a hand across his eyes. 'How was your day?'

'Mostly follow-ups,' she said. 'But I do have an operation tomorrow you might like to sit in on; the baby has a hydrothorax which is compressing the lungs. We did all the work-ups today as well as a high-resolution ultrasound and echo, to see exactly what's going on.'

'So what's making the fluid form in the baby's chest?' he asked, intrigued.

'In this case, we're not sure,' she said. 'I've ruled out anaemia or a cardiac problem.'

'What are you going to do—a thoracentesis?'

She shook her head. 'In nine out of ten cases, after you've drained the fluid, you get a recurrent build-up. A thoracoamniotic shunt—a catheter in the baby's chest which drains fluid into the amniotic sac—will stop the hydrothorax and decompress the chest so the lungs can develop properly.' She spread her hands. 'Obviously there's the usual risk with foetal surgery, that the mum will go into labour: but the baby's twenty-nine weeks. I'm giving the mum steroids to mature the baby's lungs, and we'll do it under sedation tomorrow.'

'What happens to the shunt at the birth?' he asked.

'We take it out, though the baby might need intubation and respiratory support, and possibly a chest tube for a few days to keep draining fluid. But once the shunt's in place we'll check it every fortnight to make sure it's working properly. If it gets blocked, we just redo the shunt.'

'It sounds fascinating,' he said. 'What time are you in Theatre?'

'Nine,' she said.

'I'm on a late shift, but I'll come in to watch,' he said. He glanced at his watch and kissed her. 'I know I'm being horribly rude, but I'm tired.'

'You're not being rude. You stayed late at the hospital,' she reminded him. She stroked his face. 'Or you could stay.'

Part of him desperately wanted to agree.

But he wanted their first time back together to be special. And when he wasn't half asleep. And when he didn't have to get up early for work, the next day; he wanted to savour waking up with her in his arms. 'Hold that thought,' he said. 'Because I'd love to wake up with you. But on a day when we can take our time about it.' He held her gaze. 'We're going exploring on Saturday. And we're both off on Sunday. Maybe,' he said, 'we can go out to dinner when we've finished exploring, then go back and sit on my balcony with a glass of wine. And I'll make you breakfast in the morning.'

'Saturday night,' she said, and kissed him. 'It's a date.'

Angelo was still thinking about Saturday night when he walked to the hospital, the next morning.

'Someone definitely got out of the right side of bed today,' Lidia said with a grin. 'And you're three hours early.'

'I'm going to watch Sam's operation,' he said.

'Hmm,' Lidia said, but her eyes crinkled at the corners.

Watching Sam work was fascinating; she

had the ultrasound on to guide the movements of her surgical instruments, and deftly fitted the tiny shunt to the baby's chest. She talked the team through every move she made, and the reasoning behind it, and at the debrief afterwards she barely needed support from him on translating the medical terms.

Once Giannina Gallo was fully awake after sedation, Sam sat down with her and her husband Enzo.

'I'm pleased to say the operation worked very well,' she said. 'I'd like to keep you in for the rest of the day, but if all's well you can go home this evening. I'd like to see you every two weeks for the rest of your pregnancy for a scan, to check the shunt is still working as it should be. There is a possibility it might get blocked, but if that happens I'll redo the shunt.'

'But it worked,' Enzo checked.

She nodded. 'I could see from the scan that the fluid's already started to drain from the baby's chest.'

'Thank you.' Giannina took Sam's hands. 'If you hadn't done the operation, our baby wouldn't have made it.'

'It's what I'm here for,' Sam said with a smile.

'If we have more babies in the future,' Enzo said, 'will they have the same condition?'

'It's very unlikely,' Sam reassured him. 'Now, is there anything else you'd like to ask? The last thing I want is for either of you to worry.'

'No. Last night and this morning were awful. I kept thinking the worst. But now...' Giannina smiled. 'Now, I feel as if the sun's shining again.'

'Good.' Sam patted her hand. 'I'll take you through to the ward, and get you settled in. But if there's anything at all worrying you, talk to one of the midwives—and ask them to call me if they need to, OK?'

'So how are you doing, Chiara?' Angelo asked his next patient when she came in and sat down.

'I've had a bit of a headache all morning, and I feel a bit sick,' she said. 'I took some paracetamol, but it hasn't worked. And everything's a bit blurry.'

A red flag went up at the back of Angelo's head. 'Let's take your blood pressure,' he said, 'and I'll see if I can find something to help with that headache. Whereabouts is the pain?'

'Here.' She rubbed the front of her head.

'OK. Have you been sick at all?' he asked.

'No.'

Her blood pressure was up on the previous reading, and although her temperature was fine her heart rate was a little fast for Angelo's liking.

'And you're feeling the baby kick as normal?' he checked.

'Not as much as normal,' she said.

Another red flag.

'Are you OK for me to examine you?' he asked. At her nod, he checked her over; her uterus was soft, but she winced when he touched the area beneath her ribs on her right side. And he noticed that her legs and fingers had some mild swelling.

'I'm a little bit concerned,' he said. 'I'd like to do some blood tests, and admit you to the ward.'

'Is something wrong with the baby?' Chiara asked. 'Is that why I'm not feeling him move so much?'

'I think you might have pre-eclampsia,' he said.

'But—isn't that something you only get if you're really fat or over thirty-five?' Chiara asked, sounding shocked.

'It happens in young mums, too,' Angelo said. Chiara was twenty-two, and because her periods had been irregular she hadn't realised she was pregnant until she was twenty weeks. 'We don't know exactly what causes it, but it's to do with the blood vessels in your placenta.'

'Can you give me something to make it stop?'

'The only cure is delivering the baby,' he said.

'It's too early—he's meant to be thirty-six weeks, but because I didn't know my dates we're not really sure,' Chiara said, looking distraught.

'He's got a good chance of doing well, even at thirty-six weeks. When babies are born early, sometimes they struggle a little bit with breathing, but we can give you some steroids to help mature the baby's lungs.' Angelo re-assured her. 'Once I've got your blood results back, we'll know exactly what we're doing, but you're very likely to have the baby either today or tomorrow. Can we call anyone to come and be with you?'

Chiara shook her head. 'My mum's a pan-icker and she'll just make things worse. The baby's dad isn't around any more.'

'A friend? A sister?' he suggested.

'My best friend's at work. She won't be able to get the time off. There's nobody,' she said.

It was tough enough to have complications

during pregnancy, he thought, but to be on your own as well…

He took the bloods and sent them off. On the ward, he settled Chiara in and introduced her to Emilia. 'Emilia will look after you today,' he said. 'And I'll be back to see you after clinic.' He gave her an antihypertensive to reduce her blood pressure, administered steroids and set up a magnesium sulphate infusion to reduce the risk of Chiara having an eclamptic fit.

'Emilia, can you catheterise her and keep an eye on her urine output, please?' he asked.

'And if it's low, call you,' Emilia said.

He nodded. 'And if you can put the baby on CTG—Chiara says the baby hasn't moved as much today.'

'Any signs of foetal distress, I'll let you know,' Emilia said.

'I've sent her bloods off. When the coagulation screen's back so I know what's going on, and her blood pressure's under control, it's very probable that I'll take her to Theatre.' He grimaced. 'She's on her own, poor kid.'

'I'll spend as much time with her as I can,' Emilia promised.

Angelo had just made himself a mug of instant coffee in the staff kitchen, filling half the mug with cold water so he could drink it straight down, when Sam walked in.

'Are you OK?' she asked. 'You're looking a bit out of sorts.'

'I've just admitted a young mum with pre-eclampsia,' he said. 'She's on her own and hasn't got anyone who can be with her. I'd keep her company myself, but I have clinic.' He shook his head crossly. 'I've given her steroids, antihypertensives and mag sulph, and I'm waiting for bloods to come back.'

'I've only got paperwork for the rest of the day,' she said. 'I can take a break now and finish it later. Come and introduce me to her, and I can sit with her until you're ready to take her into Theatre.'

'Are you sure?' Angelo asked. 'This is above and beyond.'

She shrugged. 'It's fine. If she's sitting on her own, worrying, it's not going to help with her blood pressure, is it?'

'I really appreciate this,' he said.

He introduced Sam to Chiara, and after his clinic had finished he checked Chiara's blood results. As he'd expected, there were raised levels of liver transaminases, urate and creatinine, and her platelets were at the lower end of normal.

The CTG results showed that the baby was

starting to be in distress, but thankfully Chiara's blood pressure had stabilised and he was able to take her straight to Theatre to deliver the baby. The little boy was absolutely fine, and when he accompanied Chiara back to the ward her best friend was waiting for her.

Relieved that she wasn't alone, he went down to Sam's office, where she'd said she'd be catching up with her paperwork.

'Baby boy, good weight for thirty-six weeks, and he didn't need any help breathing,' he said.

'That's great.' She smiled at him.

'Thank you for what you did. That was kind.'

'She's a nice kid. I hate it when our mums don't have any support,' she said. 'And my paperwork could wait.'

'Her best friend was there when I took her back from Theatre,' he said. 'How did she know Chiara was here?'

'Between us, Emilia and I persuaded Chiara to send her best friend a text, and her friend came straight after she finished work,' Sam said. 'So at least Chiara will have some support now.'

'Thank you,' he said.

'No problem.' She smiled. 'You supported me this morning. I'm just returning the favour.'

He risked stealing a kiss. 'I'd better get back to the ward. See you tomorrow morning.

On Saturday morning, Sam walked over to Angelo's flat. He greeted her with a kiss. 'Ready to do some exploring? I've got a bag with towels.'

'Are we going to the coast?'

'Not quite,' he said. 'But I think you might enjoy what I have in mind.'

He drove them through the Val d'Orcia; the roads were lined with cypress trees, and everywhere she could see vineyards, olive groves and cornfields.

'I know this is being greedy, considering how gorgeous the views are here, but I always thought there were huge fields of sunflowers in Tuscany,' she said.

'There are. But the best time to see them is the end of June. I'll definitely add them to our list.'

They stopped in a little village overlooking the valley, and walked through to the main square. Sam stared in surprise: the whole of the central square was taken up by a large pool. The water was a clear green, and there was steam rising very gently from it. 'That's not just a pond, is it? It looks like the Roman baths in Bath,' she said.

'That's exactly it,' he said. 'The piazza was built over the source of the hot springs here, and apparently it was on the pilgrim route. Although you're not allowed to bathe here in the town square, you can follow the springs down the cliff and sit in them.'

'Now I know why you brought towels,' she said, smiling. 'Great idea.'

They walked down the path by the cliff; the water beside them was turquoise and sparkled in the light. Sam bent down and dabbled her fingers in the water. 'It's gorgeously warm.'

At the bottom of the cliffs, they sat on the edge of the pool and dipped their feet in the water, enjoying the sunshine.

'It's amazing to think people have been doing exactly this for hundreds of years, here,' she said. 'The more time I spend in Tuscany, the more I'm falling in love with the place.' And back in love with Angelo, though she wasn't quite ready to say it.

When they'd had their fill of the pool, Angelo drove them to a vineyard, where they had a tour of the vines and then tasted some of the different produce; and they took the long, scenic route back to Florence.

Angelo dropped her back at her flat. 'I'll shower and change,' he said, 'and then I'll come and collect you for dinner.'

He'd made a reservation on a rooftop restaurant where they had a view of the sun setting over the river; then they walked hand in hand back along the river.

'Come and have a glass of wine on my balcony?' he asked.

She nodded, butterflies swirling in her stomach. This wasn't just wine. This was moving their relationship on to the next stage—and putting the past behind them.

They didn't even make it to opening the bottle; as soon as he closed the front door, they were kissing, and he was scooping her up in his arms and carrying her to his bed.

CHAPTER TEN

AFTER THAT NIGHT, 'taking it slowly' was out of the question. Sam and Angelo spent alternate nights at each other's flats, went for a run together before work, and spent as much time as they could together outside the hospital.

Towards the end of June, Angelo drove Sam into the countryside. 'Right. From here, close your eyes and no peeking—even when I stop,' he said.

'Got it.' Obviously he wanted to surprise her with a gorgeous view, she thought, but she did what he asked and kept her eyes closed.

He parked the car in what she assumed was a lay-by. 'Keep your eyes closed,' he reminded her.

She heard his door close and hers open; he unclipped her seatbelt, stole a kiss, and led her out of the car.

'OK. You can look, now,' he said.

And the view completely took her breath away.

There was a massive field of sunflowers in front of her, all their faces turned towards her. Behind the sunflowers, the hills rose up, crowned by a walled town and its castle.

'This is stunning,' she said. 'I've never seen so many sunflowers in one place.'

Angelo looked pleased. 'You did say you wanted to see sunflowers, and this spot's famous for it.' He kissed her lightly. 'Turn round so the sunflowers are behind you, and I'll take a picture for your mum.' He took a snap on his phone.

'And now one for your dad.' She beckoned to him to stand beside her; once his arm was round her, she took a selfie of them smiling.

'This is perfect,' she said. 'It doesn't get better than this.'

Halfway through the next month, Angelo was catching up with paperwork when one of the ultrasound team knocked on his door.

'I'm doing the twenty-week scan for one of your mums, and there's a problem. I'm not happy with the way the baby's left hand looks—I think some of the fingertips are missing—and the left foot looks swollen.'

Angelo frowned. 'Do you think it's amniotic band syndrome?'

'I'm not sure. The senior radiographer's on a break. Would you mind taking a look?'

'Of course,' Angelo said. 'But I'd like to bring Sam Clarke in as well—if it is amniotic band syndrome, she'll know and she'll also be able to do something about it.'

'Sam from the Foetal Medicine Unit?' the radiographer asked. 'I haven't met her, but I've heard she's very good.'

'She is,' Angelo said. 'Give me a couple of minutes, and I'll come down.'

He went to see Sam. 'Got a minute?'

'I've got clinic starting in ten minutes,' she said. 'So, if you're quick, yes.'

'One of my mums is having her twenty-week scan,' he said, 'and the ultrasound team isn't happy. The baby might have some fingertips missing on the left hand, and the left foot looks swollen. It could be amniotic band syndrome. They've asked me to come and have a look—and I think this might be one where you could help.'

'OK. I'll come down as soon as I've asked Carla to apologise to my first parents and let them know I'll be a bit late,' Sam promised.

In the ultrasound department, Angelo

greeted Amara and Tino Albano, then introduced them to Sam when she came down.

Sam looked at the screen, asked the radiographer to check a couple of things, and then turned to the Albanos. 'I think Gianni's right, and you have amniotic band syndrome.'

'What's that? I've never heard of it,' Amara said. 'Did I do something wrong when I was first pregnant?'

'No. It's absolutely not your fault,' Sam reassured her. 'We don't know why it happens, but the inner layer of the amniotic sac has been damaged at some point.' She grabbed a piece of paper and drew a diagram. 'There are two linings in the amniotic sac; it's like a balloon being blown up inside another full balloon, and between them is a sticky substance that fuses the linings together by the time you're sixteen weeks pregnant. Sometimes they don't fuse together properly, and bands form on the inside lining. They're really thin strands of tissue.' She indicated the screen. 'Can you see those tiny, tiny white threads?'

Tino nodded. 'What does it mean for the baby?'

'Because the baby's moving around in fluid, the amniotic bands can sometimes tangle round the baby and restrict the blood flow.

Gianni picked up that the baby's left foot looks a bit swollen and some of the fingertips on the left hand are missing,' Sam said. 'From the look of the scan, there's still blood flow to the foot—the nerves are the last things to be damaged, and if there's blood flow it shows the nerves aren't irreversibly damaged and we can do our best to save the baby's foot.'

The Albanos looked utterly shocked.

'So our baby might lose his foot?' Tino asked. 'But you said you could save it. How?'

'I'm a surgeon in the new foetal medicine unit,' Sam said, 'and I operate on babies inside the womb. Obviously, with any surgery in the womb, there's a risk that your waters could break, Amara, and at twenty weeks your baby's too little to make it.'

'But if you don't operate, our baby will lose his foot,' Amara said slowly. 'And could the bands tangle round his neck?'

'It's very rare,' Sam said, 'but yes.'

'How does the operation work?' Tino asked.

'I'd do it under a general anaesthetic and make an incision in Amara's abdomen, and then two tiny incisions in her uterus so I can put a camera in one and a cutting instrument in the other. And then I'd cut the band to release the baby's foot,' she said.

'If you do it, we might lose him. If you don't

do it, he'll lose his foot,' Amara said. 'I...whatever we do, it's bad.'

'I'm sorry. It's a horrible situation,' Sam said. 'But please let me reassure you that it's nothing that you've done wrong. It's not genetic, and it's very rare—it's highly unlikely to happen in a future pregnancy.'

Amara put her face in her hands. 'I don't know what to say. I can't think.'

'Don't make a decision now,' Sam said. 'Talk it over. Take your time. And, although I'm in clinic this afternoon, you can get a message to me via Angelo and I'll come down as soon as I'm not with a mum-to-be and I'll answer any questions you might have.'

In the end, after another meeting with Angelo and Sam, the Albanos decided to go ahead with surgery, and to allow some of the team to view the operation. The next day, Sam reassured the Albanos before Amara was anaesthetised, then went to scrub in and brief the team.

'I'm using tiny instruments, to reduce the risk of breaking Amara's waters because I don't want her going into labour,' she said. 'Obviously operating in a womb means we're operating in water, so there's movement and we need to take extra care. What we're doing is cutting the band round the baby's foot. I'm putting two incisions in the womb—one for the camera, and one for the cutting instruments. Angelo's going to sort out the camera while I do the operation itself.'

She made the incisions, and Angelo inserted the tube with the camera.

'Now we can see the baby. And you can see the amniotic bands inside the womb—those white strings,' she said. 'Can you show me the baby's left hand, Angelo?'

He manipulated the camera so she could see the baby's left hand. 'The thumb's fine,' she said, 'but three of the fingertips are missing. It's not the whole of the fingers, so the baby should be able to manage just fine with a little support as he grows up.' She turned to Angelo. 'We need the left foot, now, please.'

The white band around the baby's foot was much more visible.

'If we leave the bands as they are, they'll tighten and amputate the baby's foot,' she said. 'So my job here is to release the foot, and with luck the swelling will go down and the foot won't be badly affected.'

She pulled the band away from the baby's foot; then, careful not to nick the baby's skin and cause a bleed, snipped through the band with the tiny scissors. 'Done,' she said.

She closed up, checked the baby's heartbeat, then debriefed the team while Amara was in the recovery room. Once Amara was awake, Tino by her side, Sam went in with Angelo to talk to them. 'I'm pleased to say the operation was a success,' she said. 'You lost some amniotic fluid during the surgery, Amara, but the baby's heartbeat is nice and strong.'

'I'd like you on bed rest here for the next five days, so we can keep an eye on you. If you're worried about anything, call the midwife and they'll get hold of me or Sam,' Angelo said. 'We'll do another scan tomorrow, to see how his foot's looking, but in the meantime try to relax.'

Thankfully, the next day, the scan showed that the swelling in the baby's foot had gone down considerably, and his heartbeat was still strong; Amara was able to go home four days later.

In the middle of July, Ric asked Sam to come in for a quick chat.

'Sam, thanks for making the time to see me,' he said. 'There are a couple of things I'd like to talk to you about. Firstly, we'd like you to give a presentation to senior management next week, about the work you've been doing here.'

'Of course,' she said.

'Secondly, your secondment's due to end next week. We're delighted with the way you've settled in to the team, and we'd like to offer you a permanent position here.'

Which meant she could stay here, doing the job she loved, with Angelo,

They'd said they would see how things went, put the past behind them... But neither of them had had the courage to bring the subject up.

If she went back to London, she'd be going home to a job she loved just as much, with the added bonus of a promotion and starting the research project she'd been looking forward to. She didn't want to turn that down.

How could she choose between them?

'Ric, I really wasn't expecting this,' she said. 'I'm flattered. Really flattered. But please can I have a bit of time to think about it?' She needed to discuss it with Angelo, and find out what he wanted for the future. If she turned down everything she'd been offered in London and then discovered that Angelo wasn't sure she was what he wanted, she'd be left high and dry.

'Sure,' Ric said. 'No pressure. Maybe you can give us your answer after the presentation. But we like your work and we definitely want you.'

She thought about it all day. Angelo was working late, so she went back to her flat and called her mum. 'I need your advice, Mum,' she said. 'Ric has just offered me a job here.'

'I'm not surprised they want you to stay in Florence,' her mum said. 'But I thought you were only there for three months, until the funding came through for your research project? Or has that fallen through?'

'It's still going ahead,' Sam said. 'But I don't know what to do, Mum. I mean, I really want to work on that research project. And it means I'll be a consultant. But I'm happy here in Florence, too.'

'Would you be staying for the job, or for Angelo?' her mum asked.

'That's the big question,' Sam admitted. 'Angelo and I… We haven't really worked out where things are going with us. And I know I'm being a coward, not pushing him to talk about it.'

'Not talking is why you split up in the first place,' her mum said. 'I think we all learned from Dominic that we need to be open and honest about things. You need to talk to Angelo— *really* talk to him—and work out what you both want.' She paused. 'What do you want, Sam?'

'Everything,' Sam said wryly. 'I want Angelo and I want to work on the research project in London.'

'Can he move back to London with you?'

'Not with his dad's situation.' She filled her mum in swiftly. 'He can't really move, can he? So I can't have everything. It's Angelo or London.'

Her mother sighed. 'You need to talk it over together. Make a list of pros and cons. Think about what you're prepared to compromise on and what you're not.'

'Do I go with my heart or my head, Mum?' Sam asked. 'On paper, I know London is the sensible choice.'

'There's a huge "but" in your voice. I think you've just answered your own question,' her mum said.

'Actually, I haven't,' Sam said. 'My head says come back to London; my heart says stay in Italy. Either way, I lose something I really want. But, if I stay in Florence, I'm scared it's all going to go wrong again.'

'Talk to Angelo,' her mum said again. 'Find out how he feels. Once you've got all the facts, it will help you decide. But you've got time to make a decision. Don't rush into it.'

'Thanks, Mum.'

But, the more Sam thought about it, the

more confused she got. Did she follow her
head or heart? Or was there a middle way
where she could follow both?

Later that evening, Angelo called round to
Sam's flat. 'Everything OK?' he asked, not-
ing that she looked unusually frazzled.

'Yes—and no,' she said. 'Ric's asked me to
do a presentation to senior management next
week, before I go back to London.'

'That's a good thing, isn't it?' He looked at
her. 'Wait. He wants you to do the presentation in Italian?'

She nodded.

'I'm pretty sure your language skills are
good enough to cope, but if you need a hand
with any of the vocab while you're prepping,
give me a yell.'

'Thank you,' she said. 'I was hoping you
might be at the presentation, too, in case I get
stuck on any questions.

'Of course I'll be there,' he said. 'Though
you won't need me.' But he could tell there
was something she wasn't saying. 'What's the
not OK bit?' he asked gently.

'It's not a bad thing. Just… I need to make
a decision. Ric's offered me a job in the new
unit,' she explained.

So there was a reason for her to stay in Florence, besides him.

Which brought them to the thing they still hadn't talked about; they'd both ignored the ticking clock, wanting to see how things went between them before they had the really important conversation.

It looked as if their hands had just been forced.

Though he absolutely couldn't put any pressure on her. If she stayed, it had to be because she wanted to be there, not because she was trying to please him. 'Are you going to accept?' he asked, trying to keep his voice as neutral as he could.

'I don't know,' she said. 'I've been thinking about it all day, and I talked to my mum.'

'What did she say?'

'Make a list of pros and cons, talk to you and be honest,' she said.

He smiled. 'That's one of the many things I've always liked about your mum: her common sense.'

'She likes you, too. Well.' She wrinkled her nose. 'If I'm being honest, she *used* to like you.'

'Until I made a massive mistake and hurt you,' he said. 'In her shoes, I'd be the same. And I hope I can make things right with her as well as you.' He paused. 'So I assume you've made a list?'

She nodded. 'Where my career's concerned: if I go back to London, it's to a promotion and to a research project I'm dying to work on. If I stay here, it's swapping my current job for the same one, just in a different hospital.'

'That makes London the logical choice,' he said.

'So you're saying I should go back to London?' Her eyes widened.

He knew what she was really asking: did he want her to stay here for his sake? 'Sam, I don't want to get in your way. You have your career to think of. You've worked hard, and I'm not going to be selfish and ask you to turn down something I know you really want to do.'

'So you don't want me to stay.'

'That isn't what I said,' he pointed out. 'I just don't want to complicate your decision. You need to do the right thing for you. If you were going back to exactly the same job as you're doing here, then I'd say stay. But staying here would mean a sideways move and turning down something you've worked hard for.' He looked at her. 'This is the conversation we've been avoiding.'

She nodded. 'This decision doesn't just affect me. So I'll be brave and ask you for an honest answer: what do *you* want?'

'I want you,' he said. 'But I want you to be happy. I don't want you to stay here for my sake, then end up resenting me in the future because of everything you've had to turn down to be with me.'

'But if I go back to London, what does that mean for us?' she asked. 'You've got your dad to think of. You wouldn't have a problem finding a job in London, but you can't leave your dad.'

And his dad wasn't going to leave Italy.

He wanted to run with his heart, but for her sake he needed to work with his head. 'I think,' he said, 'we need some time to work out what all the options are and which one is the best for us. When do you need to give Ric an answer?'

'Next week. And I need to talk things over with my boss, too, to see what the options might be in London.' She looked at him. 'But the bottom line is, you can't leave your dad—and I wouldn't ask you to do that. If anyone had asked me to leave Dominic to cope on his own while I went hundreds of miles away with them, I would've said no. It's too much to ask.' She paused. 'So that gives us two choices: either I stay here with you, or I go back to London without you.'

'It's my turn to be brave and ask for an honest answer. What do *you* want?' he asked.

'I want you—*and* my research project,' she said. 'But that's greedy. I can't have both.'

'Are you sure about that?' he asked. 'Not about what you want, I mean, but whether you have to choose? There might be some room for negotiation.' He looked at her. 'We're juggling Rome, Florence and London. Maybe we'll have to spend some of the week apart, but our hospitals are twinned. Does your research project all have to take place in London?'

'That's where the funding is,' she said. But her face brightened. 'Though you have a point. I'll talk to Will and see if at least some of it can be done here.' She looked at him. 'But I want to be with you, and I want to work on that research project.'

He wrapped his arms round her. 'If your boss says no, find out what the barriers are, and we'll find a way round them. Because I want you, and I want you to do the job you love.' He kissed her. 'I love you, Sam.' He'd never stopped loving her. 'I want a future, with you.'

'That's what I want, too.' She smiled. 'I love you, Angelo.'

'Then we'll find a way to make it work.' He kissed her again. 'Together.'

This was their second chance. And they weren't going to let it pass them by. They could make it work, couldn't they…?

CHAPTER ELEVEN

SAM SPENT THE week negotiating with Will and Ric, working at the hospital and practising her presentation in front of Angelo. Early on the afternoon of the presentation, Pia Bianchi came in for her elective Caesarean.

'You made it to thirty-three weeks. That's fantastic,' Sam said, giving her a hug.

It was probably the most crowded delivery room Sam had ever been in: three midwives, three neonatal specialists, the anaesthetist, Angelo and herself, as well as Tommaso being there to hold Pia's hand and cut the cord.

The babies were all good weights: two point one-five kilograms for the recipient twin, two point zero nine for the singleton, and even the donor twin was one point nine-eight. And, considering they were premature, they all had good Apgar scores.

Pia and Tommaso were smiling through tears of joy as they cuddled their babies.

'That's brilliant,' Sam said. 'Well done. And can I be really cheeky and ask a favour?'

'Of course,' Pia said.

'I'm doing a presentation to the senior management today. You were my first patients, and it would be so lovely to show everyone a picture of you with the babies so they could see what a difference the unit made to you.'

'Use my phone,' Tommaso said, 'and I'll send you the picture. And good luck with your presentation. Tell them from us, we think you're brilliant.'

Sam laughed. 'Thank you. I will.'

'And we were thinking,' Pia said. 'We'd like to name the twins after you—Angelo and Samuele.'

'That's so lovely,' Sam said, a lump in her throat.

When Pia and Tommaso had gone with their babies to the special care unit, she looked at Angelo. 'All those weeks ago, the odds were really against the babies. And now they're here, all safe. Days like this don't get any more perfect.'

'We'll definitely celebrate tonight, after your presentation,' he said. 'I have a bottle of something nice chilling in the fridge.'

'I'll hold you to that,' she said. 'In the meantime, I have notes to write up, then I need to go home and change.'

'Me, too,' he said. 'See you at the presentation.'

Angelo was halfway home when his phone shrilled.

He glanced at the screen and his heart missed a beat. Why would his uncle be calling him at this time of day?

'Tio Sal, is everything all right?' he asked.

'Angelo, your dad's in hospital. He collapsed in the street,' Salvatore said.

It took a few seconds for the words to penetrate. *His dad had collapsed.* 'I'm on my way,' he said.

But, when he checked the train times to buy a ticket online, he discovered there was a problem with the line and the trains to Rome had been cancelled for the rest of the day.

Which left him with no choice: he'd have to drive.

And it meant he'd have to let Sam down.

He swiftly typed a text while he hurried back to his flat.

Dad collapsed and is in hospital. Trains all cancelled so have to drive. Sorry can't make presentation. Will ring when I get to Rome. Sorry to let you down, but you'll be fabulous. xx.

He slid the phone into his pocket, ran the rest of the way to his flat, grabbed his car keys and headed for Rome.

When Sam got out of the shower, she saw the notification on her phone screen. She flicked into the message and scanned it. Oh, no. Angelo must be frantic. She typed back.

Take care. Hope your dad is holding his own. Let me know if I can do anything. Don't worry about anything here. xx.

She finished getting ready, then went to see Ric in his office. 'Angelo can't be here for the presentation,' she said, 'so can you help with any questions if I get stuck, please?'

'Of course,' Ric said. 'You look worried, Sam. What's happened?'

'Angelo's dad has been taken to hospital, so Angelo's had to go to Rome,' she said. 'I'm assuming he'll call you as soon as he knows what the situation is.'

'I'll arrange cover for him in the meantime, so at least he doesn't have to worry about making it back to the ward by tomorrow,' Ric said.

'I'll message him now, while you're checking through your slides. If there's anything you need, come and get me.'

'Thank you.'

Sam uploaded her files and ran through the presentation swiftly, double-checking that everything worked; then she slipped out into the corridor to check her phone. There were no updates from Angelo, so she sent him a text.

Phone on silent. Thinking of you. Doing presentation now. xx.

When she went back into the lecture hall, it had filled up. Ric came on stage to introduce her; she took a deep breath, reminded herself that she knew her stuff and she had support if her language skills let her down, smiled, and went through the presentation.

At the end, she brought up the photograph she'd taken of the Bianchis and the triplets. 'The very first case I told you about—the mum with triplets and twin-to-twin transfusion syndrome—made it to thirty-three weeks, and she came in today for an elective section. I'm pleased to say that all the babies are doing well in neonatal special care, and I'd like to introduce you to Tommaso, Angelo and Samuele Bianchi.'

Everyone applauded, and then it was time for the questions and answers.

As soon as she could excuse herself from the drinks reception, she checked her phone. There was still nothing from Angelo. Maybe he'd been stuck in traffic—or maybe things were really serious with his dad. She didn't want to call him, in case he was still driving or talking to a medic about his dad's condition, but at the same time she didn't want him to feel abandoned. She texted him.

Presentation went well. Hope your dad's doing OK. Call me if you need anything, even if it's stupid o'clock. Love you. xx.

Ruggiero was sitting up in bed when Angelo walked in.

'Dad!' Angelo hugged him. 'I'm so glad to see you like this. I drove here, expecting you to be flat on your back, on oxygen or worse.'

'Sorry for worrying you.' Ruggiero looked sheepish. 'Sal should've called you back and told you I was fine and not to come.'

'You're *not* fine, Dad. Sal said you'd collapsed and you'd been taken to hospital. Even if he'd called me again, of course I'd be here to see you for myself.' Angelo hugged him again. 'What happened?'

'I slipped on the stairs, and it set my back off. I was going to take ibuprofen to try and calm it down enough so I could get to see my doctor. Except there was a bottle of codeine at the back of the drawer and...' Ruggiero shook his head. 'I'm sorry. I only took one. I was on my way to see my doctor. Obviously my blood pressure must've dropped a bit, thanks to the codeine, because the next thing I knew I was in an ambulance and the paramedics had called Sal.'

'Oh, Dad.' Angelo wasn't sure whether to be more worried or angry.

'I made a mistake. I won't make another,' Ruggiero said firmly. 'I'm going to take the rest of the codeine to the pharmacy to get it disposed of safely—or I'll give it to you, if you feel you can't trust me.'

'We'll sort it out,' Angelo said. 'Now I know you're OK, I'm going to talk to your doctor.'

The doctor confirmed that they'd run tests to check there wasn't something more sinister causing Ruggiero's collapse; his blood pressure was back to normal, and they were happy to send him home.

Relieved, Angelo went into the corridor so he could call Sam. He saw her messages and his heart squeezed; typical Sam to be warm and concerned, even though he'd let her down.

And that 'love you' made him stop feeling so miserable and hollow.

And it was good to know that the presentation had gone exactly as he'd expected. Hopefully the board liked Sam enough to agree to the proposals the two of them had put together over the last week, in consultation with Sam's boss and his own.

He called her. 'Hey. So you were a superstar, then?'

'I was just myself,' she said, 'but it seemed to go down well with the board. More importantly, how's your dad?'

He filled her in on what had happened. 'He's well enough now to be discharged, but I want to stay in Rome for a few days, just to keep an eye on him.'

'Absolutely.' She paused. 'Angelo, I probably shouldn't have this conversation with you by phone, but I've been thinking about it all evening. I know we had plans, but right now they're not going to work. We can't spend half our time in Italy and half our time in England, because you'll be too far from your dad if anything happens. He needs you and you can't leave him.'

Angelo went cold. Please don't let her be breaking up with him, in a horrible echo of what had happened last time; then, he'd been the one to walk away, but now it seemed that she was the one walking away. He leaned against the wall, not quite trusting his legs to hold him up. 'What are you saying?'

'I'm saying,' she said gently, 'that we need to put *us* on hold. Not for always, but for now. Right at the moment, your dad needs you and I'm only going to distract you. So I'm going back to London.'

No. *No.* This wasn't what he wanted. At all. He dragged in a breath. 'You're walking out on me?'

'No. I'm giving you space to help your dad sort things out,' she said. 'Remember, I've been there with Dommy. Several times. It's hard when you're helping someone through a relapse. You don't need someone else demanding your attention when you have to concentrate.'

Angelo disagreed. He needed *her*. But she sounded implacable. How was he going to get her to change her mind, if they weren't even going to be in the same country?

'Sam, please don't go back to London before I'm back in Florence. At least let me see you before you go,' he said.

'There's no time. My flight's tomorrow,' she said. 'You know I was always going back to

London tomorrow. Just… I'll be staying there for a bit longer than we'd planned.'

How much longer? For good? He couldn't bring himself to ask that.

'We'll find our way back to each other, if it's meant to be.'

This definitely sounded as if she was bailing out on him. Trying to let him down gently.

He needed to be with his dad, but he also needed to be with Sam. And he couldn't split himself into two. There had to be a way round this. There just had to be.

'Sam. I love you,' he said, desperately wanting her to know that he didn't want to break up with her. 'I want to be with you.'

'I love you, too,' she said. 'That's not in doubt, Angelo. I promise.'

'Then don't give up on us,' he begged. 'Please.'

'I'm not giving up on us. I'm giving you *space*,' she said.

He didn't want space. Not when he'd found her again. But arguing with her on the phone wasn't going to solve this; all it would do was make both of them miserable. 'I'll find a way round all this,' he said. 'Just don't give up on me. I'll find a way.'

When he ended the call, it felt as if all the weight of the world sat on his shoulders.

He went back to the ward, where his dad sat

waiting on the bed, fully dressed and ready to go.

'You look as if the bottom's just fallen out of your world,' Ruggiero said.

He could be brave about it, or he could tell the truth. 'It has.'

Ruggiero frowned. 'What's happened?'

'Sam's going back to London. Without me.'

Ruggiero looked shocked. 'Without you? Why?'

Because you need me and I can't split myself in two.

But Angelo couldn't bring himself to hurt his father by saying it so bluntly.

Or maybe it showed on his face, because his father winced. 'Is this because of me ending up in hospital today?'

'No,' he fibbed.

'Angelo.' Ruggiero frowned. 'Be honest with me.'

Angelo raked a hand through his hair. 'All right, then. Yes. Sam and I thought we'd worked out a compromise—that we'd spend half our time in Italy and half our time in England. Our hospitals are twinned, so we could've worked together. We'd got agreement in principle from our bosses, and she was going back to London to work out the details. But what happened today made her realise I can't live in London even part-time, Dad.' Sam had been right about that much. 'It's just too far away from you.'

'I can *manage*,' Ruggiero said. 'This was a minor hiccup.'

'I know you can manage, Dad. I'm not saying you're too weak to fight the addiction. But there are a whole host of other things that could happen,' Angelo pointed out. 'You might slip on some ice and break your hip. Or you might get pneumonia during the winter. Something that means I'd want to be there to look after you. I need to be near you. Which means I need to be in Italy, not London.'

'I can manage,' Ruggiero repeated stubbornly. 'Don't sacrifice your life for me.'

'You might be able to manage with me being hundreds of miles away,' Angelo said, 'but I can't. You're my dad. My closest family. If I go back to London, I'll worry myself sick about you every single day. Which is nothing to do with the codeine,' he added swiftly, before his father raised that particular objection, 'and everything to do with the fact you're getting older. And if Sam and I are lucky enough to have children, I want them growing up seeing a lot of their *nonno*. I can't do that if you're in another country. The alternative is that Sam has to give up everything she worked for in London—her promotion and the research project she really wanted to do—and stay apart from her family. It's not fair to ask her to do that. I mean, I know she'd do it, if I asked her, but I'm scared that years down the line she'll regret it and she'll regret me.'

'She might not,' Ruggiero said. 'If she loves you and wants to be with you, that's the most important thing.'

'Mum moved to Italy for you,' Angelo said. 'Tell me honestly—did she ever wish she hadn't?'

'No. Even when she was ill. She wanted to be here, with me,' Ruggiero said.

'Would you have moved to London for her?'

'She never asked me,' Ruggiero said.

'That isn't what I asked you, Dad.' Angelo regarded his father. 'Hypothetically and honestly. If Mum had asked you to move to London for her, would you have done it?'

Ruggiero was silent, clearly considering it. In the end, he sighed. 'Yes. I love Rome—but I loved her more.'

'Then I'm going to ask something of you, something that's difficult because I know how you feel about Rome,' Angelo said quietly. 'I want to be with Sam. Her life's in London. But I don't want to leave you. London's too far—even Florence is too far, if we're being honest about it. I need to find a compromise, something that will work for everyone.' He paused. 'So would you consider moving to Florence?'

'Moving from Rome.' Ruggiero looked thunderstruck.

'Living near us,' Angelo qualified. 'I don't want to take away any of your independence, so I'm not insisting that you live with us. But if you had your own place near us, so if you needed us we could be there in ten minutes—would that work for you?'

Ruggiero blew out a breath. 'Your mum's in Rome.'

'Mum,' Angelo corrected, 'is in your heart, and mine. She'll be with you whether you're in Rome or Florence.' He took a chance. 'Or London.'

'London,' Ruggiero repeated.

'The way I see it,' Angelo continued, happy to leave the seed of the idea of moving to London in his father's head, 'her grave's a place to take flowers, but Mum's with me every day, because I'm part of her—just as I'm part of you.' He took his father's hand. 'I know I'm asking you to uproot your life for me, and it's a huge thing to ask you. But the only way this is going to work for all of us is if we're a family. Together.'

'Have you discussed this with Sam?'

'No,' Angelo admitted. 'But I know Sam. If it works for me, it'll work for her.'

'We might not even like each other, when we finally meet,' Ruggiero warned.

Angelo grinned. 'More like the pair of you will gang up on me. Just think about it, Dad. Or help me find a solution that works for everyone.'

Ruggiero hugged him. 'You're the best son I could wish for. And I know you're trying to balance this so everyone wins. Let me sleep on it. I need to come to terms with things, my way.'

'I'll wait until you're ready,' Angelo said. 'For now, let's go home.'

The next morning, Ruggiero was already making coffee when Angelo came downstairs.

'I was born in Rome, and I planned to spend my life in Rome and be buried in Rome,' he said, and put a mug of coffee in front of his son. 'But if moving to Florence—or London—means that you have the kind of love with Sam that I had with your mother, then I'll move.' He patted Angelo's shoulder. 'As you said last night, you're part of me and you're part of your mother. And I like the idea of seeing my grandchildren grow up instead of relying on video calls.' He paused. 'I've been thinking about it.

It's not fair to make Sam's parents be the ones who have to travel to Italy every time they want to see the grandchildren. And I have your mother's family in England, as well as you.'

This was more than he could've hoped for. 'You'd move to England?'

'If your mother had asked me,' Ruggiero said, 'I would have moved for her. And you, as you so eloquently told me last night, are half your mother. If London works for you, then I'll live in London.'

Angelo could hardly breathe. 'You'll live in London.'

'You asked me to help you find a solution that works for everyone. This is it. In London, Sam gets her promotion and her research project. You have the love of your life and a job that makes you happy. And I…maybe for me it's a clean slate. A place to make new memories,' Ruggiero said.

'Oh, Dad.' Angelo hugged him. 'I can't believe you'd do this for me.'

'For all of us,' Ruggiero said. 'As long as Baffi comes, too.'

'I'll take you to visit him every day in quarantine,' Angelo promised.

'He won't need to be quarantined. He's microchipped and vaccinated,' Ruggiero said. 'I just need to sort out a pet passport. When does Sam's plane leave?'

'Lunchtime.'

'Better hope you don't get stuck in a traffic jam. I added cold water to your coffee, so drink it down and go get your girl.' Ruggiero handed Angelo a couple of cereal bars. 'Normally I would say you should have a proper breakfast, but you can eat this on the way. Now *go*.'

'I love you, Dad,' Angelo said. 'Thank you.'

He called Sam from the car, but her phone went through to voicemail. Maybe she was in the shower, or she was on the train in an area where the signal was spotty. 'I love you,' he said. 'I've talked to Dad, and I'm pretty sure we have a workable Plan B.' A perfect Plan B. 'I'm on my way to Pisa airport. Meet me by the baggage check-in.'

The journey seemed to take for ever. And when he ended up stuck in a traffic jam, he felt as if he was going to explode. Of all the days to be stuck in traffic, this was the worst. Sam still wasn't answering her phone. 'I'm definitely on my way,' he said. 'Don't set foot on that plane until you see me. Please.'

Finally he managed to park, and he ran all the way to the check-in desk.

Sam was there, glancing at her watch as

if worried that she'd either miss him or miss her plane.

And suddenly the world felt back in balance: because she was here, right by his side.

He picked her up, swung her round and kissed her.

'That's not goodbye,' he said. 'It's *arrivederci*. And there's a difference.'

'I know. And I'm not bailing out on you,' she said. 'I'm just giving you space, until you've sorted things out with your dad. How is he?'

'A lot better than yesterday. Well enough to talk about Plan B,' he said. 'Plan A was juggling Florence, Rome and London. It didn't work. But Plan B does.'

'And Plan B is…?'

He grinned. 'London.'

'But how? You can't leave your dad.'

'I'm not leaving him. He's coming with us,' Angelo said. 'He'll live far enough away from us to have his independence, but near enough so I'm not worried about him all the time.'

She frowned. 'I thought you said your dad would never leave Rome?'

'We talked last night, more honestly than we ever have,' Angelo said. 'I asked him to help me find a solution that works for everyone.' He paused and wrinkled his nose. 'I might have promised him grandchildren. Which I know I should've talked to you about first, so I apologise.'

'You're safe. We're still on the same page,' she said. 'But are you sure about this?'

'Always,' he said. 'Where you are—that's where I want to be. London works for all of us. I can get a job, you get your research project and your promotion, and we'll need to juggle a few lists while we work out where we're going to live and where we're going to get married.'

She coughed. 'Did I just hear the M word?'

He looked at her. 'Ah. I missed a step. Rewind.' He dropped to one knee, took her left hand and drew it to his lips. 'Ignore the fact we're in an airport. We're in some gorgeous gard—'

'It doesn't matter where we are,' she cut in. 'Just as long as we're together.'

He grinned. 'Samantha Clarke. You're the love of my life, and we've already wasted two years. So let's cut to the chase. Will you marry me, have babies with me and grow old with me?'

Sam smiled. 'Yes.'

EPILOGUE

Two years later.

ANGELO STOOD WITH his arms round Sam's waist, looking through the kitchen window to their garden in Muswell Hill. 'It doesn't get better that this,' he said. 'The perfect summer Sunday afternoon. My dad and yours manning the barbecue, your mum and Louisa making a fuss of the baby, Nina with Lily resting against Bump and Joe reading her a story—just like I hope we'll do, in a couple more years—and…' He spun her round and kissed her. 'And my chance to have five minutes on my own with you.'

She kissed him back. 'We're supposed to be getting the salads and another bottle of wine, Dr Brunelli.'

'It's not as if salad's going to burn,' he pointed out with a grin. 'Are you sure you're ready to go back to work tomorrow?'

'Yes. It's the best of both worlds: three days a week, so I'll still get to see plenty of Dommy.' They'd named Dominic Michael Ruggiero after both their fathers and her brother, reducing all their parents to happy tears. 'Though, after six months of maternity leave, I'm really missing the cutting edge of foetal surgery.'

'That pun is laser-like in its intensity,' Angelo deadpanned.

She leaned her forehead against hers. 'Poor Dommy. He's going to grow up hearing terrible puns from both parents, his godmother and all three grandparents.'

'All four,' he corrected. 'You didn't hear this from me, but Dad's planning to propose to Louisa tonight, and I'm pretty sure she's going to say yes.'

Ruggiero had met Louisa when he'd joined a group of volunteers to help set up a sensory garden, shortly after he'd moved to Muswell Hill, and their friendship had turned to dating, the previous summer.

'Oh, that's wonderful. She's lovely,' Sam said. 'And I think they'll be really happy together.'

'He's been worried about it,' Angelo said. 'That I'd think he was replacing Mum. Of course he isn't. He's just opening his heart a bit more. And I want him to be happy, not lonely.'

'I'm glad,' she said. 'And you don't regret leaving Italy?'

'Nope. Home's where you are,' he said. 'But I'm glad you came to Florence. That we got our second chance.'

She kissed him again. 'Me, too. I love you, Cherub.'

He groaned. 'You do know, since you let that slip, everyone seems to have made it a mission to buy me everything cherub-related?'

'Even down to the wrapping paper.' She laughed. 'At least you'll always know which mug is yours in the staff room at work.'

'And which desk,' he said wryly. 'The one with the paperweight, the drinks coaster, the card, the calendar and—' he rolled his eyes '—the bunting.'

'I dare not tell you what your dad's found for your birthday,' she said, her eyes glinting with mischief.

He groaned. 'I dread to think.'

'You'll love it,' she said with a grin.

'I love you. And Dommy. And our family. And our life,' Angelo said, and kissed her again.

* * * * *

*If you enjoyed this story, check out
these other great reads from
Kate Hardy*

**One Week in Venice with the CEO
Snowbound with the Brooding Billionaire
Baby Miracle for the ER Doc
Second Chance with Her Guarded GP**

All available now!